The United States Of Africa

The United States Of Africa

ELIGAH BOYKIN

ISBN: 978-1-64945-363-1   (Paperback Edition)
ISBN: 978-1-64945-364-8   (Hardcover Edition)
ISBN: 978-1-64945-369-3   (E-book Edition)

Book Ordering Information

Phone Number: 347-901-4929 or 347-901-4920
Email: info@globalsummithouse.com
Global Summit House
www.globalsummithouse.com

Printed in the United States of America

CONTENTS

DEDICATION

The author considers this a thought experiment of the grandest proportions. He hopes it proves more edifying than blaming the White Man and the White Race for everything under the Sun in the known universe; including its total eclipse. At any rate, it did appear to him it was high time to project the Cultural Imagination into the future, rather than let it remain mired in the tragic memories of a Cosmic past.

THE UNITED STATES OF AFRICA is the result of much soul searching about the nature of reality and being. I have always wondered and been curious, being as intimately aware of both the potentials and abilities of the Black Man and the Black Race as I am, why there was not more discussion about this concept in the here and now. All protests about past injustices involving Racism and its twin evils of exploitation and oppression seemed to me to be always walking up to the door of this subject without bothering to knock and find out who was there.

Well, you should know me by now. I told you I do not have to know before I will go. So I bothered to knock and found out who was there. I found out alright, with the high exhilaration of surprise, and treasures of new understandings. What you hold in your hands now is the poetic distillation of over fifty years of research and investigation.

Come on in, the waters are refreshingly fine...

The breakthrough came for me as the result of an ambulatory process. While walking about and thinking about things it occurred to me that the the riddle of chaos and unrest to be found on the African continent might well surrender to a kind of Cosmopolitan or STONE SOUP logic aligned to and spiraling out of just such a centralized concept as THE UNITED STATES OF AFRICA. When using this concept as a fresh starting point, one can then postulate a National Language, a National Government, one National Economy with a standard currency system, and a social sphere where the whole world, at least in this case, helps out the whole world.

Therefore, I would like to thank Martin Luther King, Malcolm X, Booker T. Washington, W.E.B. Dubois, Nelson Mandela, Frederick Douglass, Jomo Kenyatta, Rosa Parks, Miriam Makeba, Nina Simone, Haile Selassie, Loraine Hansberry, Richard Wright, Chinua Achebe, Eubie Blake, Louis Armstrong, John Coltrane, the honorable Elijah Muhammud, Maya Angelou, Marcus Garvey, Muhammud Ali, and Barack and Michelle Obama among countless others for this great adventure that begins here and is now yours to enjoy...

Lastly, I wish to thank my boon coons, Michael Moore, John Alexander, as well as Herman Yancy and Sterling Powell for the insights they shared with me while we walked and talked shooting the breeze...

I also wish to make, at this time, a special dedication to my father and mother, Eligah and Mattye Boykin, who are proving still to this day to be the living embodiment of Booker T. Washington's vision of freedom through Self Determination.

Eligah Boykin Jr.
December 4th, 2019

TREASURE BEYOND MEASURE

She was a flickering ray in a fog-filled room and
she filled that empty space in my heart where the
arid pain of a lonely existence made a vacuum that
no sound or rustling wind could contain and yet all
she did proved to be beyond the capacity to reward

The clouds moved in stately progression towards
dispersal and left the sky clear for a new experience
never before seen in the native point of view though
longed for in the dark corridors of the soul and the wee
hours of the night where no one can be seen or touched

All the great pundits exalted the wonders of technology
and still all the buttons pushed everywhere were not able
to eclipse or diminish the true value of companionship as the
very breath of life that makes all things possible while saving
intelligence quickens with renewed health and more sane love

She brought such simple things into his barren life that
the wonder was how it ever could have been discounted
how important everydayness was in being there and even
now how past all price was the kindly word and the gentle
given reassurance to his spirit as a treasure beyond measure

-- Eligah Boykin Jr.
September 18th, 2015

SHAY BECOMES DAY

The screen flickered with her bright learned beauty
ladled out with facts and figures for the outbound
worker and visitor from another town or abroad who
for the first time caught wind of the clouds rolling out
to seaward and mused about their portents for ill or good

She wielded her voluptuous presence with a scientific skill
designed to relay data to the viewer on a frequency in tune
with the music in her voice and a wide smile of gracious
understanding bestowed upon her viewing audience in lilting
tones that cheerfully exhorted the wonders of technology

There was generosity and a light-hearted sense of the good
natured missionary as the cheerful custodian of all useful
information fit to fill a sound byte punched home her updated
forecast with all the professional decorum of a pageant queen
giving the commencement speech to us graduates with high honors

While the light hollowed out the darkness and drew the shadows
back to the watery pooling places of the blue trickle that dropped
and fed the sap through the root to every fiber of the fruit of the
stalwart tree silently spilling forth its green leafy profusion in the
soft and gently timed explosion of natural growth Shay becomes day...

-- Eligah Boykin Jr.
July 24th, 2015

THE HISTORY AND THE MYSTERY

There They Were! All The Shakers And The Movers Of
Earth arrayed around the room over the blackboards.
There was Lincoln! There was Washington! All who
enter here, take note while they stare and beware!

We dutifully followed the lines of history with no
idea dawning that we ought to ask our learned
patrons where exactly we came into the heretofore
of all this hub-bub and hustle and bustle to admire
the laudable actions of those who brought us here
to be sold on the open market in jangling chains

Here they are! Fix the dates of these high heroes
in your mind and burn their deeds into your brain.
There's Daniel Boone! There's Davy Crockett! All
await their eligibility for the new Mount Rushmore

We barely flinch while our memories are branded with
the timelines of those who work their history upon us
in blood with the gun and the whip and instruct our
lessons now more casually with these hoary shadows
now firmly fixed in place to haunt us as the grim reminders
of that painful mystery that we inhabit inside their history

-- Eligah Boykin Jr.
August 26th, 2015

Inspired by David Reed

BETTER THAN IMAGINED

The hope was that the reject would come around
and get with the program but sunrises and sunsets
passed in gravitic conjunction with the phases of the
moon and still he had failed to lower his standards

Interested parties asserted and exhorted their beliefs
with the glowing and rosy flushed certainty that can
only come from staring at the Sun too long coming
up to that point where those dying of thirst stagger
at last with hot sand between their toes to embrace
finally the long wished for deliverance of a mirage

Down in the bowels of the imagination eternal
the reject reached for his compass in search of a
way out that was wholly his own but could not read
the red pointer on the dial for all of the darkness

Therefore he proceeded by feel and gut instinct and
the groping intuition of the tactile grasping around
and past the smell of rotten scrambled eggs whose
stinking scent rose out of the damp puddles and
cesspools reeking in lost chances until he staggered
upon the bright dream that was better than imagined

-- Eligah Boykin Jr.
April 25th, 2015

REAP THE CONSEQUENCES

Reason raised its hoary head above my every misstep
and I counted myself lucky that my tour through Blunderland
still left me with sufficient moxie to storm the citadel
of lost causes and last chances with whatever was left of all
my fingers and all my toes grasping for every foothold

Floundering and buffeted inside the mushroom cloud
were the pieces of my dreams swirling windward like white rice
and grains of wheat in an icy snowstorm stirred to spinning
as spirals of cream are known to do in steaming hot black coffee
and I barely know which way is up as I navigate left from right

Nobody was ever Lost in Space as much as I am right now
and a compass would not do much good outside the Van Allen
Belt anyway as I wonder without the vast certitude of The
Incredible Shrinking Man whether or not I will still exist once
my sins and crimes hail me a cab for a fast ride back home

Haunted as I am by the ghosts of offenses long since past I
forget the future is a closed book to all who are as I am rhyming
the same song over and over again without pause or cease in
the vain expectant hope that tomorrow will bring forth a newer
harvest than this one where I must reap the consequences

-- Eligah Boykin Jr.
September 12th, 2013

LOST AND FOUND

Ever since knee high he felt himself pressed against someone
else's space and locked right out of the room where he stored
all his valuable goods and could stretch himself without fear
of accidentally hitting some loved one next to him in their face

Nobody was making any space these days anyways although
there was plenty of ice to be purchased at the gas station and
bottled water was going for cut-rate prices along the dusty curb
where those without quarters held up signs for nickels and dimes

Every time he turned in the passenger's seat it seemed somehow
to him, he was in the wrong position for a late evening tryst and
actually should be doing the driving and awaiting a goodnight kiss
from his grateful date but she was on loan to fate somewhere else

He was just outside his own reality and missing the shining keys
to these premises that were somehow misplaced through all his
adventures and he was finding it hard to relate from this new view
being more on the outside looking in without any invite to the party

Exactly who were all these infidels bent on raiding the Holy Temple
of his earthly delights and carrying off all the available furniture not
nailed down to decorate their own fenced-in dreams as items worthy
of a long-awaited yard sale but just picked up from the lost and found(?)

-- Eligah Boykin Jr.
July 13th, 2015

FRONT STREET

According to all appearances the newly minted young breed
came fresh off the presses and bound for glossy renown
knew all the angles giving them over to their best advantage
and all the right catchphrases and buzzwords to burst that
profit margin up over the steep hill of mechanized uniform
mediocrity and into the upper realms of surplus heaven
surpassing all the expected gains in the dizzying and airy
climate piercing through the clouds and spiraling into
that zone where the hard copy has yet to be extracted from
its wrapper and all new shoes have yet to lose their shine

More than ever the denizens of the future generation found
themselves left to their own devices and prone to reject
a cultural legacy that impressed them as being more a form
of self-induced mass-produced blindness than a gift bestowed
to arm and prepare them for the coming trials of Life in the wild
slums of misunderstanding thoroughly imprinted upon their brows
with quizzes cunningly calculated to narrow the mind and the eye
to devices and tasks better suited for mice and robots and slaves
and yet aware that even now they were not being made privy to the
whole story ground their lens to behold a new view of an old mystery

-- Eligah Boykin Jr.
March 24th, 2015

Storage

'X' MARKS THE SPOT

He returned to the scene of many crimes unsure of where
the most infamous incidents occurred and who the parties
involved could possibly be and yet the red smears on the walls
faintly reminded him of acts he labored vainly to forget hoping to
put behind him all the past he kept reliving as an endless nightmare

Conscience drummed images into his psyche in a never-ending
staccato of guilt that rumbled through his timorous unrest with
a thunderous booming that seized and snatched him out of all his
quietude until he found himself running naked through the airy night
without knowing where he was now awakened or asleep on his numb
feet

While he shivered in the early morning wind, he became aware
that he was bereft of more than his clothes as he clutched at his
bare skin and realized that among his most cherished possessions
that was obviously revealed to be missing were his dignity and pride
and that youthful confidence in the provision and endowment of grace

Everything new was headed into the explosion zone to fly apart in
pieces no matter how benign and inauspicious the beginnings might
be crafted with the brick and mortar of honorable fellowship and rich
good feeling as he searched around gingerly for where he might have
left
the treasure chest scanning anxiously for that place where 'X' marks
the spot

-- Eligah Boykin Jr.
December 11th, 2016

A MAN WITHOUT A REAL

Everything came into view within his mind's eye
but despite the height of the tower of his reason
he found no admittance into the Halls of the Real
for all his haunted flights of imagination

The Human Parade passed him by on either side
cradling and carting home bagged game
and surplus fruit to be strained and canned in mason jars
for those late-night refrigerated raids of stored preserves

He found what he wanted always across the street
or waiting shining behind thick expectant glass
and sometimes waving at him from billboards on high
with naked feet and pearly white smiling teeth

Around him swirled the availability of every delight
awaiting his approach that he might kiss the next
door to be slammed in his face and taste that particular
grain of wood against his puckered bruised lips

Nowhere he cast his eye did he find a vacant space
where he could fling the coils of his net wide enough
to haul in those treasures of the heart gleaming green
but for the vain grasping of a man without a real

-- Eligah Boykin Jr.
May 11th, 2017

A PRAYER FOR AFRICA

O, Mighty Christ!
Muhammad!
Buddha!
Confucius and Lao Tzu!
Aesop and Mansa Musa!
Deliver us out of the snares and spiritual traps
set by our oppressors and bless us to fly free of all
those thought matrices human and divine designed
to fetter our souls

Bring us home
to the land of our forefathers
in the height of our sanity and intelligence
and the health of our love for all those beautiful
treasures of prosperity rooted in our return to that
clime where our thought was not encased within the
skin of the snake!

Let the force
of momentous endeavor work
its way throughout all the nations of Africa
and organize in spiraling exaltation the richness
of every resource human and material toward the
formation of a world power complete and whole in
all its parts

Never forsake us
and shower us with all
the signs that portend the flourishing
of the Future the planet has yet to behold
in our approach to the sovereignty of self-created
nationhood that finds us playing that grand, old-world game
of our own design!

Let us find
once again peace and security
within our own shores and the
acceleration of cultural development
that reveals itself in the free association
and friendly relationships with visitors to
and of this planet who seek to enrich themselves
within our African consciousness

-- Eligah Boykin Jr.
July 3rd, 2017

A THOUSAND LIVES

A thousand lifetimes
would not be too great an expense
or an improvident investment
considering that one is drawing from a
fund of eternity
and you might be able to do an awful lot
of good besides
with that kind of time and life experience
to work with
and who knows, but a few things might get done, too.

Discovering the secret
of eternal youth would be a worthy place to start
considering the merits
granted to lively energy and passion industriously applied
but wisdom comes
through the gradual and studied attrition of advancing years
the wear counts
and the acquisition of knowledge has yet to entirely
efface its impression
but Jazz and Baseball will find its place amongst a thousand lives...

-- Eligah Boykin Jr.
December 20th, 2017

ACCEPT NO SUBSTITUTES

Mind-boggling were the options
and alternatives presented with all the available inducements
of this year's brand of eye candy
and what appeared to his mind and vision as a simple solution
met the wall of cultural censure
and fanned out through the sieve and the prism of experience
to leave him grasping at straws
that retreated through inviting open doors to suck his energy
into the standard mirages
of national obsession complete with a cherry on top
and a free ticket
to the merry-go-round spinning the magic trick that inevitably
returned him to where he started

The haunting continued throughout storefront windows lined
with sparkling trinkets
that blinded the eye and made the forsaken stumble around
in a brilliant light
that served as a natural barrier pouring out images
tacked onto photons shimmering
salvation that was not to be touched but only endlessly
approached on numb feet
or while crawling around on all fours until there were holes
in the knees of your pants
and the skin was rubbed raw from your shaking fingertips
and the sweat rose
like rejected dew from the palms of your hands until you
steeled your will and decided
once and for all that now was the time to accept no substitutes

-- Eligah Boykin Jr.
April 30th, 2017

AFRAID TO LOVE

Looking at Life through the prism
of his own fear and frustration
he was unaware of the peculiar tint
his own backed up feelings of rage
and hatred gave to everything he viewed
through the lens and rain of pain and suffering
that pelted him on all sides coming at him unanswered
and without the possibility of eventual redemption

Nestled among his peers here he was sequestered
in hidden resentments and unexpressed hostilities
that defined him while the gathering crowd outside
his window taunted to him to come out and fight
and show what kind of pinata he was made of
so that each duly approved member of the community
could take their appointed whack at his dreams now
chipping and flaking and breaking to pieces like fine china

How long was he to stand at the threshold
while these acquaintances barely more than strangers
stepped through to their just desserts and headed
onward and upward to God knows where
but at least it could be said of them they were not
standing still or spinning their wheels in the rut
of human endeavor aiming for nothing and going nowhere

Now all the things he dreaded to do
came flooding into his senses
as doors, he once thought of as locked
but which the wind was harshly revealing
as merely closed awaited that daring impulse
of the one who would step past his petrified shuddering
and the dividing line that separated the rightful victors
from those poor souls who were yet afraid to love

-- Eligah Boykin Jr.
March 16th, 2017

AFRICAN GENIUS

The force of it came forth out of eyes now blind
and loins ungirded long ago according to the will
of the sporting castrator and it stood outside the back
doors of restaurants now reserved for those whose privilege
paled before the natural rights of those in ascent to their destiny

Foaming and percolating in between texts of history
as casual as the unnoted breath were these invisible
figures of truth unknown to the many and yet moving
inexorably to a grand culmination like the stately procession
of clouds gathering rank and file before the coming of the storm

Invention pressed its way into these souls darkened
in degradation and woe and delivered unto them means
and measures with which to resist and triumph and in the
most startling encounters their lips would even know the nectar
and taste of the wine of success plowed and cultivated from their toil

No one sensed the logic of it all rooted in every spiritual
doctrine since time began and even the greatest puzzle
master seemed asleep to the fact that the pieces were all there
and ultimately must fit into a pattern and design for freedom that
would awaken the whole world to salute the power of African Genius

-- Eligah Boykin Jr.
May 21st, 2017

AFRICAN REGENESIS

We pride ourselves on how well we play the games
of White Men while praying fervently to play a game
of our own invention that will make us Champions of the World

We hit the books with baby powder producing a fine white
mist of atmosphere that will coat everything according to the
history of these affairs gluing back the page we took from their histories

We lacquer our being with images of design alien to our nature
as we strive to make our very protons take on and conform to the
properties of electrons dancing in the magnetic flux of the Western Way

We stand in line holding our tickets and waiting to be summoned
next in order that our forms might be approved sparing us the trials
of dismemberment and immolation slated for the unreconstructed
outcasts

We apply ourselves assiduously to the study of everything except
ourselves and rehearse without cease to be called up and appointed
to the role of this season's buffoon for the night in the palace of the big
bucks

We are strangers to our own success and unwitting abettors to the
decay of civilization as we know it while glimmers of insight flash
behind our closed eyes and beckon to us to be what we once knew we
could be

We recoil from the brightness of the light unused to it as we have already
adjusted our eyes to these dim quarters and find comfort and uncertain
solace
within the cocoon and beneath the dissolving mantle releasing African
Regenesis

-- Eligah Boykin Jr.
June 11th, 2017

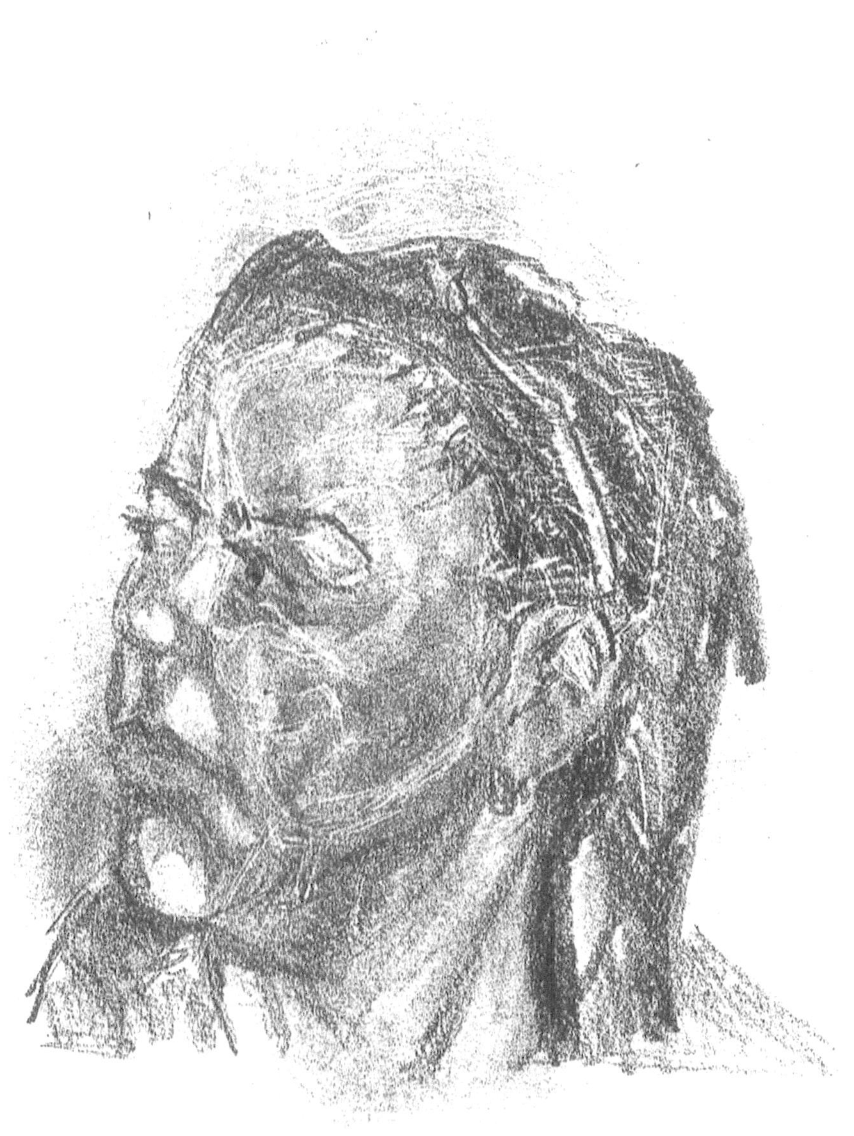

AGENTS OF LIFE

Many insisted that the correct marker to observe
was the force of death
as it worked its entropy through the manifold and
sundry structures of cells
banded together to promote those forms without
name and number known
in the circles of the learned as living things on the down
cycle breaking away and
deteriorating into the delusion of the end of strife and
muting suffering into silence

However, at the fringe of the howling mob cheering
and smacking its lips
for the gore to be ladled on even more thickly now
into the swirling soup
of hot blood kindled in the flames of passion
were those who spotted
something stirring in the ground and breathing through
into the green radiant
summit of the encompassing blue space a whisper unseen
amidst the agents of life

-- Eligah Boykin Jr.
December 19th, 2017

ALGORITHMIC UNREQUITED LOVE

Down in the basement of the poor house he could be found
wrestling with his demons just off the beaten path and outside
the concourse of well-meaning folks now upholding the traditions
of a polite society mired in the quicksand of indebtedness to one and
all who began believing before violently awakening to the deceiving

Events began so benignly while those pale with advantage
kept up the chant of equal opportunity until even the keenest
observer was hard put to tell what the left hand was doing as the
right hand was thrust forth out of those angry clouds offering some
sentiment of friendship complete with jangling chains and a missing key

About mid-course he began to sense the shape of things
to come and go in an opposite and reverse reaction that none
of those at the top enjoying the icing would be subject to anyway
albeit he was finding himself groaning to shoulder the cares of the
world and could liken himself to Atlas or to Christ as he might choose

The ruts of experience trenched him into predetermined
paths of resistance that led to all the same old places where
self-command disappeared with the waning Sun and he was left
standing in the dark of a hope and a wish extinguished time after time
all after her inviting smile vanished to reveal algorithmic unrequited
love

-- Eligah Boykin Jr.
January 12th, 2017

ALL THE ASS YOU CAN KICK FOR FREE

Many thanks to Astaqul C. for the title!

The young man gave a broad grin
and commenced to eat cheese
into old age
promising to be on time
and to cross all t's and dot all I's
but the cookie he ate upstairs
in the principal's office
after making it onto the honor roll
could not compare to
all the ass you can kick for free

Our hero wandered the wide and narrow
trails of Earth and meditated
in distressed confusion
about the error of his ways
each probing step of his journey
seeming to head to nowhere
and yet there awaited looming over the horizon
the treasures of a lifetime
flickering for the taking and
all the ass you can kick for free

Hard to study the contrasting views
of Martin Luther King and Malcolm X
when unknown classmates
insist on stealing your books
and you are torn between the methods
of men of peace and those of men
who reach up ready to take arms
but for every young man there comes a time
when enough is enough, and you are ready to settle
for all the ass you can kick for free

When the bait and switch is on
and for all intents and purposes
you can see a line winding around the block
of folks holding onto their numbers
for their turn to punk you out and give
you the pussy whopping that comes
with a lifetime warranty
how can you not crave a way out
when both cheeks are red
and you are finally entitled to
all the ass you can kick for free

-- Eligah Boykin Jr.
October 31st, 2017

APPROVED BY GOD

We came across
a band of bushmen
and called out
across the Kalahari Desert
hoping that one of these
robed worthy fellows
could show us
the way to Gaborone
but our cries and shouts
brought no echo
nor in any way
checked their stride
over the grassy plain
as they advanced single file
under the hot, dry sun
to plow and to plant
for the coming harvest
or herd and graze live meat
at the cattle posts
before these are butchered
at the abattoir in Lobatse

After the first rains came
the Exodus
from the dusty towns and villages
and rounded thatched huts
to those places
past the hunters with poison-tipped arrows
and the buffaloes, elephants, and lions
on roam in realms never frequented
by Queens Victoria and Elizabeth
peering blankly from the blue stamp
of the Bechuanaland Protectorate
where

Seretse and Tshekedi finally work
the Bamangwato chieftainship
into that shape and place
where even Ruth
could find herself
a part
of a Commonwealth of Nations
approved by God

-- Eligah Boykin Jr.
February 2nd, 2018

ARMIES OF SPIRIT

We are as red ants
scurrying upon a hill of sand
for all our reason
unable to buy even another day
in eternity despite our
most abstruse calculations stirring
down here in the Cosmic
swirl of things

The fighters pound their way
into the ash heap of history
having no knowledge that can
revoke their ticket back
into the enfolding void
and handle life with all
the muscle and impact
they can muster

The lovers exhale and exclaim
at every opportunity to glimpse
the impulse of life renewing
itself around every corner
where a kiss and a caress
a hard-pressed hug and a
fevered cuddle somehow lead
to a filled stroller

The creators stumble through the nebulosity
of their vision blindered more
than the one-eyed man
who once was king
before he lost his crown
and swore to revenge
himself on the faceless hordes he found
sentenced to the slaughterhouse

The destroyers clamored for more
fodder to shove through
the meat grinder of human offense
and barely blinked beneath
the pelting red rain of blood bursting
open the cloudy nightmare
to reveal unexpectantly the triumphant
armies of the spirit

-- Eligah Boykin Jr.
September 11th, 2017

ATOP THE GREAT PYRAMID

Frederick Douglass arrived at Giza
and decided to make the climb
here in the cradle of Civilization
where the Ottoman Turks rode
the heady wind of conquest to Empire

Standing there on that plateau
among the wonders and the ruins
of the Metropolis of the Dead
he began the climb upwards
many stories above the Valley of the Kings

The ascent was no more rugged
then his own life in bondage
proved to be until he found the courage
and the strength to hold
that would be slave master Covey at bay

And so in that hot desert climate
he found himself atop the Great Pyramid
of Cheops forty-seven stories up
and sat as Narmer might have reflecting
on that home of his once owned by Robert E Lee

-- Eligah Boykin Jr.
April 13th, 2018

BASEBALL AND COMICS

Strange the things that come happen on the block
while you are eating popcorn
with your feet up in the Admiral Theater
and watching James Bond beat them down
on the Orient Express
in between thumbing through
the monthly adventures of THE AVENGERS
and sweating out how to draw comics the Marvel Way
with Kirby making it all look more simple
than Al Kaline hitting the winning run in the ninth
but who would have thought beginner's luck
would surrender to the wizened experience
of the seasoned pro smelling the victory that comes
at the end of a Louisville Slugger

That poster of Doctor Strange looks good
pasted against the ceiling of a makeshift clubhouse
designed to lure in neighborhood girls
while the folks are on vacation down South
and Mountain Dew never tasted so fine
until you have dug out a floor two or three feet deep
by the bushel to snug in planks
so that you can float your cool rap
as you tread the boards in a home away
from the burning summer's sun and wonder
when you will ever have this much fun
snatching rubber-coated hardballs out of the deep blue sky
and hitting one over the first baseman leaping up
beyond parent's cries to come home
to the building blocks of Life
past all farewells to baseball and comics

-- Eligah Boykin Jr.
March 27th, 2017

BETTER THAN IMAGINED

He was fond of the license to limitlessness
that came with all that he imagined
and the sprouting arrogance knew to seed
the harvest of his own downfall
in due time
according to the heady intoxication
such fancies provided as he strove
for those dreams that recoiled upon him
and mocked him as time and again he came up
short
and watch the aim of his heart and soul
resolutely disappear from view

Life kept telling him that all that was needed
was for him to blow his top
and let the Sun come in
applying expert knowledge here and there
with that fighting grace and take charge thrust
that would win for him and all concerned
the transformation of the world
into a dimension whose sheen might prove
to be brighter than the polish of any advantage
of the moment
and engrave upon his life
a permanent inscription honoring all his illusions

Soon he knew the searching must inevitably
come to an end
as he finally arrived at the edge of his own understanding
and found his efforts surging furiously out of the dark
lion's share to wind up ultimately parked at the boundary
of his own limitations wanting some lift
from a hallowed unknown source
that might grant him
the benefit of its favor
and bring him home
into something better than imagined

-- Eligah Boykin Jr.
March 30th, 2017

BETWEEN THESE STONES

The land rumbles and the ghosts among
the Bouar Megaliths wonder
now trapped between crusty terror and rage
the minions of this world
servants and slaves of earthly matters
and the carnal impulses that propel
the decay of everything we seek in our
rugged and rock-strewn surroundings
who gave the French the right to establish
and define our borders since no one sent us
or our neighbors' invitations to attend
the Berlin Conference at any time before
or after the Slave Trade while the Bobangi people
trafficked in human flesh along the Ubangi river
and the students at the University of Bangui
swore in French and Sango when not set to flee
the next Civil War or returning to pick up the pieces
from the last violent rebellion achieving
the autocratic measures of Boganda and Dacko
and Bakassa as we play the ongo with the pygmies and
Banda people for the inauguration of Catherine Samba-Panza
wondering when will things get any better between these stones...

-- Eligah Boykin Jr.
April 2nd, 2018

BEYOND BASEMENT BLUES

Looking up from the bottom
of his own defeat
he saw things presented to him
in a strange phantasmagorical light
objects appearing closer than they actually were
and yet curiously out of reach
with the kind of permanence that only exists
on the other side of cultivated prejudice
and the wall of dark reflected emotion

Flecks of admiration arose from out of his
entombed soul and found there
mirrored essence in the jagged crevices of broken
and cut glass strewn across the paths of all
his immediate adventures owing
to the stripe of degradation that he bore in relation
to the color and the texture of his thought and deed
and those who opposed him relished and reveled in the success
of their carefully calculated machinations
now bearing their bounty of evil fruit

There was nothing that was more a preparation
for a new insight
a point of view that might make dreams come true
in some other place than the ruminated
Netherlands of fitful sleep and revolving nightmares
and love for those who found their profit
in spurning him and all his arduous labors stood for
as a vision slowly formed out of the murky waters
of that sentence decreed from personal folly that would lead
inevitably to that awaiting birthright of freedom

-- Eligah Boykin Jr.
April 16th, 2017

BEYOND DESPERATE VOICES

Down in the inward dungeon
the torture
of the anguished mind begins
defying the Magic of the Baka
and impelling the Bantu to move
wherever they can
to forge new kingdoms
far away from Lake Chad

Portuguese sailors found treasure
in the ghost shrimp
flourishing in the Wouri River
and Cameroon was born
to sustain the footprints
of Christian missionaries
and the Arab slave trade
as Adama led his Holy War
Ahdjo broke with France
to legislate Independence
before placing the reins
in Bya's hands
who drove the country
into war with Boko Haram
at the Nigerian border
while stewing in homegrown
corruption
at home and in the Capitol

Clashing with Nigeria over
the vaunted black gold
of the Bakassi peninsula
brought few riches
to either party while literacy soars
in French and English
and writers like Mongo Beti
analyze the scars
of Colonialism in Cameroon

-- Eligah Boykin Jr.
March 25th, 2018

BEYOND SHERLOCK HOLMES

Past the gas lights and the fog-shrouded moors and
letters written on the wall in blood along with figures
of Dancing Men promising death and grim retribution
there comes a time when even the three pipe solution is
not enough to foil and resolve the darkening of murky waters

Past Professor Moriarty and the roar of Reichenbach Falls
tumbling and spilling into the slimy depths of the whirlpool the
postmortem remains of whatever rage and repression forms and
and accumulates in the icy residue of cold, rational logic pinning foul
murder on those whose churning suffering it inevitably cannot prevent

Past Irene Adler and Violet Hunter and the machinations
of lovers mixed up in compromising situations and sundry
red-headed men auditioning and applying to read the Encyclopedia
Britannica for a living while a Spanish wife of hot blood takes her place
and stands upon Thor Bridge in her scorn preparing to blow her brains out

Past the curse of the Baskervilles, we go now down into
the Valley of Fear where Birdy Edwards proposes to rip
the mask of terror and while dodging outside the sights
of Colonel Moran, we discover much to our chagrin that Love
is stronger than death and a ratiocination beyond Sherlock Holmes

-- Eligah Boykin Jr.
February 2nd, 2016

BLESSINGS IN DISGUISE

There was nothing in between the split in the concrete at first
besides clumps of twigs and clogs of dirt wedged there in the loose
mortar and packed in tight after the rain and the snow and the wind
did their work across the stomping grounds and battlefields of the Earth

The marvel was how Life always found a way to turn tragedy
inside out in order to confer some kind of unexpected boon to
wary and watchful eyes on the alert for the final certain destination
of spiritual advantage over the detritus sifting through timely decay

These ecstasies and pleasures usually arrived in the guise
of Trojan Horses bringing the neglected and bruised harbingers
of life instead of the grim agents of death stealing themselves into
the dead of night as the dread messengers of blood lust and conquest

Seeds traveled on the wind only to be trampled underfoot
or to find entombment in a watery grave or ground fine beneath
a plot of earth or this side of a streak of tar or asphalt and moldering
and fomenting in insignificance that never foretold its own becoming

Barely beneath notice, the passerby make no report about
their progress while the Sun and Moon work their magic in
those unencumbered silences of light and darkness owed to their
orbits and revolutions unmasking in the right of time blessings in
disguise

-- Eligah Boykin Jr.
March 6th, 2017

BLISSFULFILLMENT

When he first entered the reddened folds of her trembling
he found himself driving down the newly minted Highway to
Heaven and before he knew it was renewed in every fiber of his
body and mind and soul with hair growing woolly and thick and
flourishing as knotted muscles and the pulsing plow of his manhood
finally reveling in its discovery of that virgin field in which he sowed and
planted his seed in exclamations of grateful prayers piercing through
every
oath and curse with the happy explosion coursing past the point of no
return
to land in mid-space where matters of moment dissolved into the
mystery of life

Nothing twisted itself into everything and she no longer harbored
any doubts as every argument she stored up in the back rooms of her
mind came spilling out of their bags onto the floor and sifted the air with
the fine grainy substance and fragrance of pollinated rebirth and
finally the
Earth and Heaven interfaced and recognized their reflection in each
other and
pulled together rather than away from themselves enjoying the warm
mix of their
energies in rising flux untempered in the straits of passion and
overflowing the banks
of previously established borders crumbling before the onslaught of
some unnamed
force
and vaporizing into unknown and limitless quantities to all spiritual,
sexual
blissfulfillment

-- Eligah Boykin jr.
February 2nd, 2017

CHALLENGES OF MANHOOD

He watched her sleeping in his bed and mildly wondered
at this newfound sense of security within himself as he now
basked in the glowing confidence that he could provide for her
and be the shield for her against all those things that might block
them in creating a family worthy of themselves and the world we live

Their food was a reward for a job well done and the clothes
they donned were cleaned and pressed with their own hands
and beyond the ceiling to the roof above them the entitlement
of energy invested wisely and time well spent providing insurance
for valuable service to the community as he watched their money grow

Soon skill upon skill accrued to their lifestyle and all the little
things that added nuance and texture to living increased that sense
of security one finds in accumulating knowledge and the times became
as comfortable as new pillows fluffed to fullness and tools and languages
became weapons well oiled and to be kept safe and in good working
order

The years stretched out before them, and no one could foretell
the future but their feet were set firm on solid ground due to the
foundation that was already established within their hearts and minds
and the vows of a lifetime would prove to be the ties of love that served
him well against the wheels and chains and hurtles and challenges of
manhood

-- Eligah Boykin Jr.
February 9th, 2017

CHANTS OF OBSESSION

The voices in his head
became a drumbeat
for more than he would ever know
between the coups
and the struggles for power
Lamizana overthrowing Yame'go
then ruling until Colonel Zerbo grabbed the last of
the musical chairs
and how was he to know as he
stood inline
for his vaccination that Thomas Sanbara
would not be
long for this world and that even the best
of his ideas
and policies would be overturned
but for the
Hymn of Victory in the Fatherland
of Honest People
and still, the gold and tin ore came out
of the mines
while the slaves in the Sahel toil on despite
drought and famine
and the whispers mouthed in his mind
kept him up
at night and stung him in the middle of the day
while the memory
of Gando primary school seemed to fly
on the heels
of Blaise Compaore' to the Ivory Coast
as he entered
the University of Ouagadougou past
chants of obsession
for Unity and Progress and Justice

-- Eligah Boykin Jr.
February 10th, 2018

COFFEE CEREMONY

Asmarina poured the first round
from the jebena and looking here
and there raised her eyebrows
to see who wanted more
while the cycling men flashed by
on the dry roads in bright colors past her window

The committee discussed improvements
since the Liberation of 1958 and after
a heated discussion about the size of the military
and the rise in life expectancy everyone appeared
ready for the second round of the brew to come
and to broach the subject of maternal and infant mortality

After kalaay, someone lamented the shortcomings
of a one-party state while the krar was plucked
and the wata played for all its strains with a melancholy
air that suited the discussion of illegal search
and seizure of those at odds with authoritarian rule
that left many in Eritrea mourning lost loved ones

Now came the third round of the afternoon
and the conversation grew more animated
as tongues wagged in Tigrinya about the size
of the military being unwieldy for the population
it policed and how the erratic fluctuations in the prices
of gold and silver and cement was making it hard
to economize even the coffee ceremony in these times of unrest

-- Eligah Boykin Jr.
April 14th, 201

CONCERNING SPIRITUAL LEADERS

We were all in a quandary as to how to conduct ourselves
and how to best manage our affairs when all at once he stirred
our souls and lifted our minds higher than any of our petty concerns
regarding the gains of the moment marooned as we were here in our
vast iniquity and paying in vain against the spiritual deficit of our
blindness

We would measure the rightness of each other in newfound
virtue whenever in his presence and marveled at how he could
mend shattered lives and women as well as men broken in soul
and limb found themselves restored to wholesome health through
casual contact and simple passing talk as he walked the paths of Man

We found ourselves caught up in the life-saving essence of
his energy and those throbbing with hate found themselves
transformed into loving friends somehow even while holding
a gun to his head and looked down again at empty hands bereft of
weapons as the reason to live proved stronger than any rage to kill

We caught glimpses of his vision throughout the underground
passages of our spiritual travail and coughing up the dust raised
in the reeking clouds of our transgressions felt inspired to be better
than ever we imagined in our wildest fancied flights and in achieving
this contemplated with fulfillment those goals concerning Spiritual
Leaders

-- Eligah Boykin Jr.
February 11th, 2017

CONFESSIONS OF A TIME LORD

There were places to glow and things to free
and he would free all of them and make
those special places of sanctity that were everywhere
throb with the hum and breath of peace

He sure got around as only Masters of Time can
do and when he was not jumping through
exploding doors he was diving out of open windows
quaking from the commotion of adventures all around

Times without number he could recall when he thought
the endgame was all wrapped up with a pretty red
bow unaware that the worst was yet to come as it unraveled
before his very eyes sundry events he calculated to harmonize

And lately, it was becoming hard to tell the heroes
from the villains without a scorecard as certain portions
of the populations of Earth were still prizing success
and making prayers to the God of winning at all costs

But there was nothing for it but to keep snatching
the blindfolds off everyone he encountered
as a true Time Lord should until he finally ran into a
sympathetic ear ready to hear the confessions of a Time Lord

-- Eligah Boykin Jr.
May 14th, 2017

CONFORMATION OF DIVINITY II

We deliver the heart and soul of us into all our endeavors
hoping to plug into and connect with the infinite source and
the divine intelligence that augers in the raining twinkling sparks
that provide supernatural governance for every affair of the corporeal
and the temporal and pray skyward for the reward of that helping hand

Our eyes uplifted see nothing but clouds parting and dispersing
into the blue breath that serves as an airy skin for earth and living
creatures of every stripe and kind who suck from the swollen breast
of the invisible their sustenance for every wet second of their planetary
sojourn unable to detect in the ensuing silence the coming of always
there

We run through the trees up and down the slopes of sunlight
filtering through the leaves and its shadowy domains where the
tests and trials reside in all those familiar haunts to tease and bait
us with the challenges of Life and Death amid the here and nowhere
as we clench our teeth and strain our eyes in the gathering vast dimness

And Adam takes Eve by the hand as they navigate by night
the asphalt Garden of Eden with wary tread peering askance
for those real and imaginary dangers prone to cross their path
and find their only cheer in the friendly wayfarers they are disposed
to encounter and greet them tumbling forth as confirmation of divinity

-- Eligah Boykin Jr.
January 23rd, 2017

CONJUGAL REWARD

The old man finished filling out his forms
as his prison sentence
was coming to an end and his mail-order bride
standing there outside waiting
and enduring the ogling eyes of the convicts
their whistles and catcalls
and fluttering tongues and weathering the glare of this
lustful approval in stride
clutching her purse against her bosom
as she gently leaned
against their gleaming ride parked in hover mode

The old man mentally checked off the exact specifications
of his particular order
and he could see through the six-inch glass and bars that
she met all stipulations
the presence of her confirmed to him she would meet
every condition and requirement
there was the look to her of a filled out questionnaire
each section accounted for
while he signed off for his personal items and removed the tags
filtering one last time
past the maze of armed guards and Thought Police toward his conjugal
reward

-- Eligah Boykin Jr.
December 21st, 2017

CONQUEST OF UNBELIEF

There were mirrors everywhere he looked
all around him people
up close and personal
reflections of the nature of his lush, lusty wish
a giant shadow crawling on the wall behind his
quivering form rearing up on its hind legs
ready to pounce

He stood before a wall of his own undoing
brought up short
against that thing known
to be invisible and yet permitting no penetration
into the wild realms and hinterlands of overflowing
miraculous times on tap to those whose surety
unlocked the door

Little did he know he was now back once again
digging a pit
for himself and fellow
travelers into the unknown misty breath of the
possible tracing the tips of his fingers over the outlines
of the dusty finish line awaiting at last that final
conquest of unbelief

-- Eligah Boykin Jr.
November 8th, 2017

CROSSES WORTH BEARING

Past the last treasure laid up here on Earth
many forego the rewards of the flesh and carnal
acclaim to navigate the fissures in the path that must
be tread according to a higher aim in mind for all who
bear the crushing weight and numbing pain of sacrifice

Suffering comes to all those in need of freedom
from want and the desperate needs of the soul and
the heart anchored and chained to a body denied even
the liberating flight of the sparrow much less the soaring
vantage point of the hawk spying its prey under the airy dome

Forced to wander and hew their own way out of
the sin that binds them to each other in lockstep
and single file wearing invisible chains stronger than
any kind of metal or iron dug or mined from the pits of
the Earth so we sojourn along gritty trails this prison planet

We wear our viewpoints as blinders and must plow
the narrow trough of our perspective as though bound
to it from the time of our birth and plant our seeds of love
wherever we may find in the startling surprise of unexpected
bloom that endless increase that makes all cross worth bearing

-- Eligah Boykin Jr.
February 6, 2016

CROSSROADS OF CIVILIZATIONS

Brahim Chidike arranged his millet and water
in his backpack for the trek to come
there was a long way to go
across the foothills and paths where once
Civil War was known to rage in full

He was headed for the capital N'Djamena
and even now he ruminated with thoughts
flitting between the advantages
of the University of N'Djamena and those
of King Faisal University – Chad

Brahim faced the East and said his prayers
perhaps consultation with an imam at a mosque
once he arrived at the Capital would help to ease
and clear his mind and the hovering doubts
that flapped and sniped at the edges of his soul

Reviewing mentally his Arabic and French
and his internal commitment to be
an International Man rather than an Ethnic Man
he wondered what Idriss Deby would do
to make Chad once again a Crossroads of Civilizations

-- Eligah Boykin Jr.
April 4th, 2018

DARE TO WIN

Fear crept out of the dark corners
and nipped at their sleeves and heels
and no matter where they ran it found them
cowering and seeking a hiding place
casting about for a crevice in time out of sight
from the lurking and looming menace
luring them into a confrontation that no longer
could be postponed with any diplomacy
that did not strike blows for its very own survival
leaving all social airs to scatter in the wind

Suddenly the love of a good fight
was all the rage and the standard of the day
with the victors taking all and the victims
eating the dust and the clay of the floor
as time and again Life unhooked them and threw
them back into the fray to find a purchase
on the rough ground where personal attacks were
the expected and common coin of those devoted to the
get or the gain coming over stumbling bodies trapped
in the rattling scrabble of scraping to dare to win

-- Eligah Boykin Jr.
December 21st, 2017

DIVINE INTELLIGENCE

We look upwards to the Heavens
imploring the God above all
what there is required of us
and always from within us
and without us
we feel cast down
upon our brows
the glowing rays of a smile
such
as the sunlight feels upon the bare skin
of being fearsomely naked
to the benign touch
of the one who is infinitely manifest
in our experience of Eternity

We cast our gazes across the wind
stirring shimmering waters
azure and gold light now acting
as a see-through mirror
between this realm
and the one the senses cannot touch
with all the available means
at the disposal of Time and Matter
and seek to plumb the depths
of our home-made darkness
tailored to make sure that one size fits all

We reflect on ourselves
when was the last time
we heard the call
and knew who was speaking
throughout the corridors
of our souls
as well as the inmost dwelling place
of our hearts' whereabouts neither
enshrouding loneliness
or magnanimous sight
serves to kindle any more
then a glimpse of the one
whose presence is more natural law than felt reality

We ask ourselves
what spoke to us
with such certainty
that
all else was swept aside
in order to fulfill that inner edict
such
as we beheld before us
brooking no interference
from any given quarter
here in life
or death bordering
the vaults of heaven
and the screaming torments
of hell
as we answer our connection
to Divine Intelligence

-- Eligah Boykin Jr.
January 29th, 2017

DOIN' A DUCHAMP

Fugitive whispers chased and haunted him throughout
the night and begged for an entrance into those grand
spaces that might allow for virgin conferences with newly
minted beauties surviving a final revolve on the potter's wheel
of Nature but he ignored the buzzing as they were doin' a Duchamp

Cries in the night barely found their way through the holes
in the web and still bounced back in echoing calls of ecstasy
affirmed through the interstices of crisscrossed strands that failed
to trap patterns of light filtering the darkness and he felt compelled
to close her every scream in a happy kiss as they were but doin' a
Duchamp

He felt the soles of her feet in the palms of his hands and before
he knew it was sunk down deep in the quicksand of her honey caught
as a fly would be moaning in the sweet sticky flow of all that they were and
could be waxing out of the tremors of their flesh while the shocked air
seized
them in a suspended thrill aching in forever as they were only doin' a
Duchamp

Found objects became pawns writhing and jockeying for position
in the midst of the chessboard and finding no anchor in the center
they gasped and grasped for advantage in straight lines and diagonals
while spewing blasts of pent up emotion down inflamed corridors in
search
of salvation denied the intellect since after all they were just doin' a
Duchamp

-- Eligah Boykin Jr.
May 20th, 2017

DROUGHT IN ZIMBABWE

There was a thirst throughout all the land
that fifteen years of guerilla war
could not put an end to no matter what Mugabe decreed
there was a hunger for that thing
Christ wanted when he was offered vinegar on a stick

The mouth watered and the throat went dry for it
a faint scent of it in the air
between the Limpopo River and Lake Tanganyika
a flavor not covered or provided for
under the new constitution of colonial authority

There was no clause dealing with it when the time
came for all the signers to put their
John Hancock on the Unilateral Declaration of Independence
but Robert Mugabe followed the scent
to a landslide victory launching a new nation into chaos

People went to the Zambezi River with their pots and buckets
hoping at last to sip its magic waters
but they ladled in cholera, and the AIDS pandemic dripped
from their spoons in its stead and the cry from
the people went out for the teachers to return from their exodus

-- Eligah Boykin Jr.
June 30th, 2018

DRUMBEAT

The sound of the drums
could be heard
throughout the neighboring villages
violence was brewing
in Brazzaville and Pointe-Noire
the air was full of it
and dread rode the wave of voices breaking
crying harshly in surging
crowds of protest and demonstration
hungry for constitutional reform

There was a buzz in the streets
that reminded one of the three-day uprisings
that ousted Fulbert Youlou from the Presidency
and brought Alphonse Massamba-Debat
to one-party rule
but the transfer of power has yet to prove
itself easy here in the Congo
and even 'scientific socialism.'
can find itself on the way out in a bloodless coup
that finds Marien Ngouabi
answering the drumbeat before
assassins find their way to his door

-- Eligah Boykin Jr.
April 4th, 2018

EMPIRE TO REPUBLIC

Land of Mansa Musa and the Epic of Sundiata
which tells of the Battle at Kirina
that propelled the Mali Empire into its flourishing
across two centuries
and yet these kingdoms prove to be
as mortal as the men who make them
and come undone in time as the Earth
shrugs them off like worn-out clothes

Songhai expanded into pride and power
outstripping even Mali in territory
and wealth, but the seed of its destruction
came from within after the death of Daoud
and civil war spread its legs to the invaders
from Morocco at the Battle of Tondibi
but even Judar Pasha's days were numbered
after the looting of Timbuktu and Djenne

Samori Toure brought the Wassoulou Empire
to a short life before his capture
and death, leaving a legacy of resistance
against French colonial forces for his
great-grandson Ahmed Sekou Toure
as an inspiration to build upon
in winning independence from France
but still, the flaws of men will prove
to be the shortcomings of State as even
Alpha Conde' might be forced to concede

-- Eligah Boykin Jr.
April 30th, 2018

EVERYBODY COMES TO TUNISIA

Skander stood in the ruins of Carthage and indolently
scribbled his notes in Arabic
making careful to place this scene correctly on the timeline
somewhere around the Muslim conquest
of the Maghreb, his thoughts lighting like flies upon the rotting
corpse of the invasion of Hannibal during
the recorded exploits and adventures of the Second Punic War

The mosaic of the Lady of Carthage came to him but did not find
an easy compartment within his mind
as he ambled past the eroding columns down the wide dusty
boulevards paved with the flagstones of the past
and the memory of footprints that came from many lands

Sunlight was fading, and he knew it was best to budget
his time for the fuller exploration
of the Medina of Tunis and all its monuments and mausoleums
and fountains spewing into the atmosphere
the ghosts and the shadows of the Almohad and Hafsid dynasties
and Spain seizing the coastal cities before
the Ottoman Empire brought Barbarossa and Suleiman the Magnificent
and the French forced the Bey to the terms
of the Treaty of Bado proving only once again that everybody comes
to Tunisia

-- Eligah Boykin Jr.
June 29th, 2018

EVERYTHING BUT LOVE

We traversed the widely traveled boulevards wanting for
something we could never find in the narrowed marts of
trade spelling out product value on the placards in dollars
and cents and the coveted discount advantage of renewed
patronage so honored in the Capitals of Commerce as we
find ourselves richly rewarded with more and more stuff

We entered the Citadels of Learning where students now
unknowingly bore the crosses of too much misinformation
upon their backs after the daily scourging of instructors bent
upon graduating these charges with the standard rubber stamp of
maladjustment into the Status Quo just below that contemplation
of the faintly curious and vacuous absence of something belonging

Who would have known that the young spawned out of all our angst
yet and still would see us with such clear-eyed innocence and their
role in the coming prophecy of spiritual bankruptcy and cultural debt
garnered upon those battlefields long ago converted and transformed
into cities of the dead for the greater service of all mankind pledged to
honor those promises forged from the grist of many broken covenants

Meanwhile, we numbly shuffle gathering our coats and closing
our collars against the foulness of the shrill howling wind turning
every corner past skyscrapers whose towering sides broadcast and
flicker brightly colored commercials and cheery eyed men and women
ready to solicit every longing and yearning need with the latest advance
in the new and improved putting here at our fingertips everything but
love

-- Eligah Boykin Jr.
December 5th, 2016

FACES OF CULTURE

Even here in Monrovia ethnocentrism reared
its stony visage of cultural mispropriety
amongst the indigenous peoples of the bush
and freed blacks of the American Colonization Society
felt obliged to exclude native tribesmen from their birthright

Volunteers came out of slavery to the Pepper Coast
with no fore-vision or plan to study any of
the cultures, talk or spiritual ways of those ancient
tribal Africans descended from the Mali Empire
and thus the seeds of violent Civil War were sown anew

Sparks flew and caught fire in the cultural gap
between those who knew chains and those
who knew none and the emancipated freedmen
found themselves defending their settlements
against the Kru and the Grebo secured in their chiefdoms

Nasma Zahan was having her mother mend and fix
her gown and pack her dresses and quilts for her studies
soon to come at the University of Liberia and her friend
Mulbah was rolling up his poster of George Weah having
successfully passed his examinations that qualified him
to attend the Louis Arthur Grimes School of Law...

-- Eligah Boykin Jr.
May 11th,

FIRE AND BLOOD

We were constantly being seduced
into accepting their point of view
and denying our own
distracted by the blinking lights
and the fluttering pixels
from finding out who we really are
and what our true history is
in the flux of these events of delusion
reeling and looping us into the roiling waters
of a cultural confusion masquerading
as institutions of truth and light
oblivious to the blinding darkness
these mechanisms of human society cover up
promoting the invention of ignorance
in all those areas where knowledge might serve
as food for the soul and a boon
to the violently fevered and hectically obsessed
in their productions of destruction designed
to reach a nirvana of power inside
a mushroom cloud of fire and blood

-- Eligah Boykin Jr.
December 3rd, 2017

FLOWING AND GROWING

Standing naked before each other
the room sealed off
from outside sounds and intruders
their heat and breath
was now the only thing between them
and they realized gasping
that the two of them were both open books
filled with blank pages
with nothing but bare feet and shoulders
present to recommend them

There were no shadows here to mark
the passage of time
no place to hide or retreat to in this place
the lights watched them
confront each other with their life histories
and the invented drama
of having nothing but each other to look toward
between four bare walls
with a top and a bottom supplying all their needs
for flowing and growing

-- Eligah Boykin Jr.
December 21st, 2017

FREEDOM IN MAURITANIA

There was no need to consult the marabouts
and most of those interested in the power of knowledge
were seeking higher education outside the country
beyond the Sahel droughts and famines in the mix
of juntas and coups with and without the blood of slaves

The University of Nouakcholt might one day produce
lawyers capable of enforcing laws across the vast desert
and captains of industry finally raising the standard of living
enough for those on the farm and those herding and selling
camels when not mining for copper and iron and siphoning oil

Even Moktar Ould Daddah would be hard put to say that
after the hard-won Independence from the French
the newly minted power brokers were planning to ratify
an end to slavery for all woman of childbearing age
and children without an education eligible for sweat and labor

Now the question remains will the Moors and Haratin
along with the West Africans use Modern Standard Arabic
or French and English to educate the benighted out of the belief
that slavery is a part of the natural order of things and will
one more change in regime finally bring Freedom in Mauritania

-- Eligah Boykin Jr.
June 11th, 2018

FROM THE MINARET

Idris looked down from the Minaret
while the imam went to get the tea
he could see the white camel down below
casting a pale shadow in the sand
next to the brown streak that was the road

He could see the people beneath him
going in all directions the way ants go
the blue compact in front of every one
and everything and the little tree wearing a
green leafy crown growing out of the barren ground

Under its shade there ought to be an oasis
he mused to himself, but there was no water
down there even as the droughts would come
and go and then leave the soil without any
will of its own to even grow another tree in sight

But that was the way things went here in Niger
empires would arrive and depart with the French
and Sundiata Keita and there would always be
too many babies dying and too many being born
and the only thing he could think about when the imam
brought the tea was how more people needed to learn
how to read and write and see the view from up here...

-- Eligah Boykin Jr.
June 20th, 2018

GHOSTS OF THE COAST

Momo called on Eneida to go with him
to the local cinema
Mortu Nega was now playing there
and this was not the time to pass up
the work of the internationally acclaimed
Flora Gomes making history for his countrymen

Now that independence was here one could
calmly glide along on the sound
of the calabash in the airy night as the couple
swayed to the beat holding hands
and passed quietly in the dark before
the mural of their hero Amilcar Cabral

The two sat in the darkened theater where women
brought their babies to breastfeed
amid their cries, everyone was staring up
at the flickering screen depicting the War
for Independence and the drought that left
a dry taste in the mouth and spirit

No one made a sound as it became clear
how witheringly somber was the journey
of its stars, their actions highlighted in blood
and the fighting of rebels going down good
with rice and sweet potatoes wrapped in wax
paper and the thirst for freedom seldom quenched
since Guinea Bissau was bound up with the Mali Empire

-- Eligah Boykin Jr.
April 30th, 2018

GRAND MARRIAGE

Hamada prayed for Allah to be merciful
sweating out the expenses
for increased social standing
in English pounds
by the thousands
and despite the grace and beauty
of his beloved
whose aspect went quite well
with the dazzle of gold and jewelry
it was hard to hold back the curse
under his breath, as he calculated
the suffocating bride price
he would be due
simply for the right
to stand first in line at the mosque

He came from nothing
hauling in the nets of fish
with his father
and slowly working his way up
on that vanilla plantation
between coups and the musical chairs
of Presidents for the Independence
coming and going like some sweet fragrance
exuded from the yiang-yiang vine
until finally, he made it to Moroni
and borrowed enough for the Mna Dabo at least
but who in all of Comoros made it so
that his full rights as a man would one-day count
on something as bankrupting as this Grand Marriage?

-- Eligah Boykin Jr.
April 4th, 2018

HAPPY ACCIDENTS

When her feet met the concrete
she did not expect to be swept
into a whirlwind of amazing occurrences
that would take her breath away
and present to her the true face
of what she was all about

She did not imagine she would be
caught between two clashing modes
of nature
each pulling her in the opposite direction
torn as she was between what(?)
everybody knew she should be
to serve the common good
and the sudden interface with a shining spirit
in the throes of a personal discovery
moving at breakneck speed to the inevitable
destination
of a rich journey leaving her holding
a standing invitation to come along for the ride
over and across the lifelines
of her tremoring hands

And so the question loomed large
within her soul
now cleaved to his own
what would be the upshot of where
they were going
now that a paved road emerged
out of the detritus of their happy accidents

-- Eligah Boykin Jr.
December 15th, 2017

IMAGE OF GOD

When he considered it
in the cold light of day
he came to realize
it was not for riches or fame
that he began to write
to commit to paper and pen
the unbridled wildness of his imagination
in tales and stories designed
to thrill and amaze
no
it was all much simpler than that
he simply wanted to know
what it would feel like to be
God
and he learned more than he bargained
for
he discovered it was more intoxicating
than any drug on the market
and plied his energy and thought
for the hookup to all that
infinite bliss, infinite knowledge,
and infinite being
while Christ chuckled and pointed
and slapped Buddha on the back
"Who does that boy think he is?"
Krishna giggled and shook his head
as they continued their walkabout in the garden
and Confucius noted how the lotus flowers
were now in full bloom...
"All he has to do is come through me
and there will be no more peeing on himself
in the mean streets or boners in the middle
of the night to deliver seed into the wasteland of
vain imagination."

But to be like God!
There was more to that idea
than a poor benighted soul
saddled to a body made out of meat
and hypnotized out of fully enjoying the Eternity
that was his natural birthright could resist
and so
he kept siphoning power off the mainline
to charge himself up with that feeling of supremacy
that would let him know
when the time was nigh
to put a whupping on even Muhammad Ali

-- Eligah Boykin Jr.
August 20th, 2017

ISLANDS OF AFRICA

Long before Cabo Verde found itself
caught in the iron vise
of the triangular trade
fanning out in manufactured goods
for slaves
and the raw materials
processed and refined
to fuel the dominion
of the New World
the Phoenicians and the Moors
came to visit
leaving little evidence
to report
pardoning the oral narratives
and a passing mention
in the Nbo Lobo tales

Between the pages
of the Claridade
writers such as Tavares
and poets
the stamp and stripe of
Baltasar Lopes Da Silva
strove to make that break
from Portuguese literary thought
that would serve as a movement towards
an Independence that even
Sir Francis Drake could not challenge
and attack
no matter the waxing and the waning

among
these Islands of Africa
of drought and famine
proving less than
the machinations of Cabral and Fonseco

-- Eligah Boykin Jr.
March 25th, 2018

JOHN HENRY COMPLEX

We pounded against the system exhaling all our fierce energy
into blowing apart the whole house of cards into a clattering
roaring pile of rubble and rubbed our ashy hands and elbows
and knees deep down in the musty misty dust of everything
we prayed and hoped would be the end of all our servitude

Our contract in chains shattered at the sound of clanging
hammers on ringing steel with each blow responding in
hopping streaks of light streaming red down the trembling
bars and fingering warmth across the wooden ties as the
swinging echoes made fresh smashing sweating sparks

No time for Book Knowledge with the hot flaming breath
of oppression breathing down your neck and scorching
your pants with more heat than the last time you sat upon
a radiator and giving you the hotfoot between each spike
you drive with all your might into that good black earth

The Mighty Thor and David Bowman have nothing on you
in this classic battle of Man against Machine and in your
pumping heart lies all the will to conquer the iron and steel
tracks laid across the entire spirit of the nation and in the end
that sweet soul music bangs out a jazzy John Henry complex

-- Eligah Boykin Jr,
January 12th, 2016

LAND BEYOND MARTYRS

All the most renowned of the planet seemed to come
into fashion once they were committed to lay their bodies
down for the good fight and the just cause no matter
how lost and hopeless matters became in planting
the seeds of a new vision for the sightless in a bind

Strange how it is always a serious matter whenever
people are ready to risk life and limb and place their
lives upon the altar of a higher aim whose inspiration
appears worth the sacrifice of all available material means
and puts into play those values nobody is able to do without

But dying for something is a hell of a way to make
a living and puts flowers on coffins and tearful women
in black veils and dresses better than it does food on
the table or clothes on the back of anyone or a roof
over the heads of orphans forced to fend for their way

There are those who would argue that Death dips
the quill of history into the blood of the fallen and that
those not willing to die for something are not fit to
live, and yet there is something to be said for life
ushering in life to dwell in a land beyond martyrs

-- Eligah Boykin Jr.
September 19th, 3015

LAND OF MUHAMMAD ALI

The nightmare of Bentiu began that night in April
the poor and the indigent scrambling
for places of safety while threats over the radio sent
the dread of rape through the hearts of women
young and old as they spirited their children away

Peter Par Jiek searched through the smoke and the haze
for a way out past the flaming buildings
wandering the streets just now becoming littered bloody
with the wounded and the dying crying out
while stumbling over fresh corpses around every corner

The people of Bentiu sought refuge in their town
huddling wherever they could inside the lee
of churches and under the pews before the altar
making themselves small under the beds
in the places of healing and the frenzy of the wards

Nonetheless, the soldiers came for them in the mosques
and ferreted them out from place to place with
the bark of commands and the cracking report of gunfire
putting an abrupt stop to running footsteps
strangling screams into silence in this land of Muhammad Ali

-- Eligah Boykin Jr.
June 26th, 2018

LEADERS OF THE FREE WORLD

Long goes the dawn into morning and the shadows have a ways to stretch
before gathering unto themselves the cloak of darkness enshrouding the
the horrors and the crimes of the West in avarice masquerading as Life
and Liberty within the bloody margins and upon the besotted carcasses
of wildlife placed before the altar of sacrifice and privileged pursuit

The Sun was slowly peeking over the horizon in a glare ushering forth
the Age of Woman and the wheel was grinding exceedingly fine the
time of its arrival but would not have its hands set back even for
daylight savings time and so Eleanor Roosevelt continued now
weaving new ideas for the raiment of the worthy and the great

The Suns of Mexico stood upon the sands of the Alamo and collecting
around the local Mariachi Band envisioned a coming time when the
highest office in the land would be held and occupied by anointed
descendants of Juarez and Zapata who steered the country as a
whole to greater freedoms for hard-working Arabs everywhere

Chief Seattle sat with Sitting Bull who chided the shaman Geronimo
about his hair cut and citified clothes as the Holy Man Black Elk
admonished them to settle down while posing for this latest of
the works in sculpture rivaling Mount Rushmore as he spoke
of his vivid dream that made them leaders of the free world

-- Eligah Boykin Jr.
December 10th, 2016

LET US BE THEIR MASTERS

There is no reason to emulate those who make a mockery
of the souls they could never conquer to their fullest satisfaction
beckoning many thus benighted to follow in the footsteps they never
were able to make upon holy soil so let us now resolve to be their masters

The avatars of high technology and miraculous science zealously
promoted their latest advances in the science of the art while tremors
shook the ground beneath their feet and the sacred rug was snatched out
from underneath them proving at once it would be best that we were
their masters

Wherever the moral high ground disappeared it was safe to bet
these folks were no longer standing upon it as they sent invitations
our way that we might participate in all the available activities of their
decline while they swear in drug-crazed fornication and beg us be their
masters

Now that there were no more races to conquer what would fuel
the engine of their progressiveness since those who fell victim to
their Death Wish were resurrecting themselves with newer tools of
of freedom that would make them as fate would have it their new
masters

The trail of blood that was left on everything was now being
wiped clean by those these interlopers wronged and shuttled
into oblivion as enlightened minds of every stamp were suspending
exercises of insanity and exhorting all the oppressed to let us be their
masters

-- Eligah Boykin Jr.
March 4th, 2017

LIFE OF LIBREVILLE

We made our way through the rainforests
careful to step around the vipers
and to give the wild elephants free roam
as the villagers resentfully did
complying with the wishes of the late President Bongo

We are headed to Libreville to celebrate
Independence Day and earn a little carving
masks for the ancestors and the tourists we find
and right now keep out of the caves as my buddies
and I am done prospecting for dolomite and limestone

We heard Anthony Obama was in town
and we are looking to meet him
when he gives his lecture about his silver medal
at the University of Science and Technology
or is it that other one named after Omar Bongo

We see cement everywhere around the beachfront
but it is about time someone took down
that billboard of President Ali Bongo Ondimba
the dry season will be hot, humid and short
and who needs him to scare away the goats and chickens

-- Eligah Boykin Jr.
April 25th, 2018

LION OF JUDAH

Emperor Haile Selassie paced the halls
at Fairfield House with a thunderous heart
pondering when he might be as fortunate
as Menelik II at the Battle of Adwa
and return to the Horn of Africa
with his Faith vindicated

Often during his morning constitutional
he reflected with Kassa Haile Darge
on the pilgrimage he made to the rock-hewn
churches of the Laibela as Mussolini
and his forces attacked them in the air and
on the land with the help of the Raya and the Azebo

The prayers and the fasting came back to him
after the disaster in Tigray at the Battle of Maydew
all that was left in the failure of his counterattack
was to present his case to the League of Nations
but what could even that August body do
as now Italian troops marched their way
into the hallowed Capital of Addis Ababa

And so,
this distinguished nobleman
claiming descent from Solomon
and even the Queen of Sheba prepared
his address to defy the fascists the world over
and persevered through the trials of State
as well as the sudden blows of personal tragedy
until the Standard of
the Lion of Judah
was raised once again in Ethiopia

-- Eligah Boykin Jr.
April 24th, 2018

LITTLE LEAGUE OF UGANDA

Godfrey nodded to Bwambale once he got the sign
having no idea that he was standing
where the hunter-gatherers of his ancestors once stood
more than two thousand years ago
the most important thing now was to throw hard for a strike

Bwambale barked at him in Swahili and the hardball
thudded off his catcher's mitt
the one with the broken strap and he wrung his hands
and chuckled askance to Godfrey
enough practice might land them in the Kampala finals yet

One might study to be a doctor or a sanitary engineer
these were worthy and respectable professions
in the eyes of Ugandans everywhere when considering
that for all accounts his country was still
viewed as one among the poorest in the modern world

But on the fast track, one might make it to "The Silverbacks."
and now that Idi Amin was long gone
along with the Kingdom of Buganda that Milton Bote abolished
there just might be a place for him and Godfrey
in the 2018 Little League World Series should the Lord be willing

-- Eligah Boykin Jr.
June 30th, 2018

LIVE TO CRAWL ANOTHER DAY

Gazala picked idly through her couscous
until she caught the earthworm
in the window
out of the corner of her eye
how the creature arrived there
was a complete mystery to her
and so she meandered outside
into the green school garden
to lift the nightcrawler
gingerly up from the sill
There before the blue waters of Aguelmane Sidi Ali
she held the slippery thing
between her fingers
the fate of its segmented existence
as uncertain as that of the Pied Noirs
in her country after the Algerian War
but there in the palms of her hands
she could not see how
this quivering mass of tapering life
could offend or bring ill to anyone
and decided on a whim
to kneel down in the grass
and set it free
to enrich their native soil
and hatch its eggs
before returning to play
with the cubed and diced tomatoes
in her couscous salad

-- Eligah Boykin Jr.
December 5th

A salute to Radio Reed for the title...

LUNCHTIME IN MOZAMBIQUE

Rabia yawned as she fiddled with the pages
in her history book and looked around
at Shakil wondering what kind of lunch his mother
prepared for him today as she casually
glanced at the heading of the next chapter in her book

She wagered there was matapa in that little red bowl
with the yellow top sitting on his desk
while she idly flipped through and scanned with her eyes
the pictures and illustrations accompanying
the Mozambican War of Independence in her History lesson

Shakil looked her way and chuckled to himself knowing
what she wanted and he made a face at her
playing with the lid to his plastic bowl and hoping he could
trade some of the shrimp in his stew for just
a little of her Piri piri chicken and a good handful of fries

The Schoolmaster finished up about the War of Independence
and after muttering something sage about
President Filipe Nyusi made the whole class stand at attention
then marched them outside for the annual group photograph
while Xadrque smirked with a steak roll between his fingers

-- Eligah Boykin Jr.
June 19th, 2018

MAMADOU

Stepping out of the University of Dakar
the tribes of Senegal see Mamadou coming
armed with his weapons of knowledge
enough to heal the wounds of a nation (?)
nobody knows
in the dryness of the Ferlo or the minds
of the elders
unable to make their mark or read the messages
in the sand

What have the Wolof and the Fulani to say
when they come upon him stumbling across
the dirt roads and trails to their huts
and compounds armed with nothing but books (?)
under his arms
and a stethoscope hanging about his neck
the way
nooses do for all those plotting the downfall
of the president

How many francs would the nobles pay
to have the griots sing their praises to the name
of Carver who mined the peanut for its great wealth
to serve the ports with products for the world (?)
while miners
in the west dig for pockets of zirconium in the pits
of the earth
and Mamadou probes for the beating heart at the end of
the long drought

-- Eligah Boykin Jr.
November 9th, 2017

MILKY WHITE THIGHS

Booker T. Washington and W.E.B. Dubois were hard put to compete against her milky white thighs gliding along the riverfront in shorts upon her bike glistening in the Sun and unaware of the impression she now made and the striking image she presented before the shimmering waters of the Detroit River amongst the hustling of the milling crowd

Malcolm X and Martin Luther King could set Freedom to ring and their body and blood made for great soul food, but when you take in the sights on a lazy summer's afternoon sometimes nothing can compare to the vivid
impression made when milky white thighs cruise past pumping pedals in the cool breeze enveloped in blue sky and sunshine on the gritty sidewalk

Funny the things that register enchantment in the mind and end up filed into some secret little treasure box to be reviewed every now and then with
wistful amusement for an idle repast and there is no need to belittle or even
exalt a simple unadulterated moment of pleasure when it comes free of charge
shuttling and soaring past with all other wonders of nature as milky white thighs

Popcorn and peanuts and eye candy are unbounded treasures for the senses on
tap in unlimited amounts for the grateful spirit finding priceless satisfaction in
the simplest of pleasures flitting in the air with the aroma of lemonade and ice
cream along with sparrows and pigeons towards some agreeable perch that finds
Nature providing silent companionship in a slow asphalt roll with milky white thighs

-- Eligah Boykin Jr.
July 23rd, 2016

MORE THAN A HANDSHAKE

What did the Bantu peoples discover
here in the heart of Africa
amid its Great Lakes and rain forests
when the goods of its earth were ripe
for the taking to all interested parties

King Leopold knew a good thing
when he saw it long after
the Ete' Pygmies used their Katanda harpoons
to spear giant catfish in the Semliki river
and he did what he could to get good rubber
out of the local population
regardless of the cost to human life

What did Ali and Foreman find
when Mobutu invited them
to Kinshasa for the Rumble in the Jungle
did they hear the groans and screams
in the dungeons below
as they went toe to toe
and blow for blow (?)

What would Patrice Lumumba make
of the high hopes that floated
and flowed with the Congo river
the length and breadth of the country
finally running red with the blood
of the First and Second Congo Wars

Does Jesus weep when the thunderstorms gather
and dry his eyes in the pouring sunlight
knowing what Africa is and what it could be
beyond the greed for gain and wars designed
for those meaning to ascend
to the throne of corruption
reflecting thoughtfully how human freedom
requires
more than a handshake...

-- Eligah Boykin Jr.
April 4th, 2018

MORNING IN MOGADISHU

Ayaan heard his mother calling and drowsily got up
to say his morning prayers before
preparing for school and he struggled for the facts
he was memorizing for today's class
about The Silk Road and the Birth of Islam here

He slipped into his house shoes and did his best
to keep from scratching where his polio
vaccination was on his arm stray facts floating off
the top of his head about the silk road and
the Middle Ages leading up to Independence in Somalia

Outside his window he could see wreathed in clouds
the Mosque of Islamic Solidarity as he
stretched and did his best to stifle a yawn stacking
the photograph of Almnara Tower over
all the rest including the painting of the Sultan of Adal

After finishing up his prayers he opened his eyes
and rising from his knees rolled up
his prayer mat and stuck it back under his bed
mentally reviewing the timeline of Somalia
and the feats of Muhammed Abdullah Hassan as he
ran downstairs for breakfast this morning in Mogadishu...

-- Eligah Boykin Jr.
June 23rd, 2018

MOSHOESHOE REIGNS SUPREME

Moshoeshoe stood among the ruins of Maseru
his ghostly presence a mere wind fanning
the smoldering glowing embers of riots that for him
could only hearken back to the days of the Boer Wars
Who would come now to see the Rock Art
of the San people with this unrest
in smoking evidence all around and through
the capital towns of Mafetang and Mohale Hoek

Soon March 11 would be here to celebrate
but despite his plan to take a seat
at the National University of Lesotho
standing in this rubble brought other things to mind

How like the time of troubles this was when
the invading Nguri clans and Shaka forced him
and his people to move and settle into the stronghold
now known as the mountain of the night

The children trotted past him in alarm wrapped up
in their Basotho blankets barely aware of his presence
while he caught the whistle of the lokolulo and somewhere
women were plucking the strings of the thomo to his name

There was still time he thought to himself between
the military juntas and the coups to throw the mask
off in a whole new way not withstanding Eugene Casails
remark about the Boers and their devious ends
Moshoeshoe decided to head on foot
for the festival in Morija
where his day might be honored properly
with a little local jazz, vocal choirs and some Famo

There was still the water and the diamonds
the literacy of the people was among the highest
in all of Africa, and the Katse and Mohale dams
were enough to inspire the awe of any visiting tourist

King Letse III and the Prime Minister ought to know
what to do while even now some comely maiden
was stooping down to put fresh flowers on his grave
so that even his memory might always reign supreme

-- Eligah Boykin Jr.
May 10th, 2018

MURDER IN MALAWI

Nyasaland somehow survived the Scramble for Africa
and with the blessing of the Bantu and Queen Elizabeth
became a land around a lake one third of its size
now that the British were done with their coming
and seeing and being eventually dissolved out of town

Lumbani and Sephora descended the steps of the GO-LINER
shaking the blood back into their legs and stretching out
the Johannesburg blues now that they were setting their feet once
again upon the soil of Malawi in the Capital City of Lilongwe and could
forget about the body the tourists found while hiking Mulange Mountain

The Ufulu Festival was in full swing at the moment and how different
Kenyatta Drive seemed from Thyolo Road where they heard the gun crack
as here travelers arriving from distant lands were all hailing the local
public taxis
riding in rocking minibuses and on the Kabaza reading and exclaiming
about the
horrid news before meeting to dance and sing with the people during
the Lake of
Stars
Sephora and Lumbani made their way through the farmers market
walking past
gorgeous and juicy wares of fruits and vegetables glistening in the Sun
before them
and set upon sheets of burlap down the length of the wooden sheds -
but what were
they
to do - Chimango was a friend - and they knew his weapon must be
hidden - as they spied
visitors volunteering skills at the Lilongwe Wildlife Center - so none
would know it was he...

-- Eligah Boykin Jr.
June 4th, 2018

MYSTERY OF CLIMAX

What kind of planet was this
where it was necessary
to shield your eyes from the Sun
a radioactive ball of gas
powered at its core by nuclear explosions...

What kind of galaxy was this
spinning away from that
major event as all the rest followed
a blaze of light filtering
gas and dust through the very sieve of Life...

What kind of universe was this
grinding Time and Space
and Energy into solidities of illusion
that none can pass a hand through
or much less touch with a fingertip...

What kind of dream was this
that enfolded the void
in a geometric perfection that without protection
fell to pieces in the reaches
of far-flung space as a mystery without awakening...

-- Eligah Boykin Jr.
August 14th, 2017

NIGHTLIFE IN NAIROBI

God knows against a big Nature
the whole works of our every solution
among the question marks that are lost
in the world of our unknowing calculation

Where we would reign in Free Will
the Eternal One dwells in Faith musing
at the comings and the goings of Mzee Kenyatta
along the length of the Ugandan Railway

How well have his countrymen harvested
the bitter fruit of the Mau Mau rebellion
he wonders
as he stands before the Statue
of Dedan Kimathi
with disdain in this new Age of Independence

What brings a terrorist to the exalted state
of a National Hero in the eyes
of the Kikuyu and Kenyans everywhere as far
as Nairobi and this side of Lake Victoria

Father Africa ruminated what could Kibaki
be playing at to have this revolutionary
and all he spawned in his wake honoured
when he was barely able
to fathom
the painful evolution of Freedom in its Truth

But no comparisons with John Brown
and his American brand of fanaticism
could keep Mandela from seeking out
Kimathi's widow Mukami and her children

And so the old man sighed and shrugged his shoulders
and made his way towards the Kenyan highlands
content to disappear into the shadows of history
with nothing but the books WEEP NOT, CHILD
and FACING MOUNT KENYA
in both his hands...

-- Eligah Boykin Jr.
May 9th, 2018

NO LONGER AZAWAD

Sundiata unfolded his latest edition of Nouvel Horizon
and looked out at the Sun glinting
upon the Nile River
from the top of the Tower in Bamako
with the times of Babel in his mind

He glanced down the hallway at Fanta speaking French
and serving tea
to the Finance Officials
checking their clipboards and cell phones
for the latest graphs on gold and salt
shipping out to the ports of the world

Further down the polished floor past the clicking sound
of footsteps dying away
Sundiata could see
the elder Shakur seated behind a glass partition
and squinting
and holding a magnifying glass
up to sundry soiled pages

A descendant of the Griots of Sambala the venerable old man
carefully scanned the lines
of Sudanic script
the recollection of that time
when the Mali Empire was twice
the size of modern day France
made him smile

Sundiata watched as Shakur rose on creaking joints gingerly
placing between gloved fingers
the laminated pages
of the Timbuktu Manuscripts back
into their slip covers
and binders to return to
the University of Bamako
thankful that in the North Mali was
no longer Azawad

-- Eligah Boykin Jr.
June 10th, 2018

NO MORE BLOOD DIAMONDS

Rebels found the diamond region in their hands
and traded the rough stones for guns
and weapons that would win their cause somehow
until the United Nations stepped in to stop
the traffic in precious gems and armed guerilla strife

Civil war came to an end and left millions cast out
with nowhere to go even to bury their dead
or grope with the buzzing flies for a place through
the thickening fog of their grief and between
the savanna and the rain forest for a place to rebuild

Fatu and Amad returned to school in Koindu astonished
to find it was no longer there and looked around
to walk through the buildings without doors coughing
on the faint scent of smoke still trailing away from
the holes in the walls where the blackboards shattered

The students stepped gingerly over the rubble looking
for where their desks used to be and textbooks
fanned their pages in the breeze giving them fleeting
glimpses of their assignments about Bai Bureh
and Ernest Bai Koroma as stumbling forward they found
a path between the church and the mosque that led
possibly to Freetown and no more blood diamonds...

-- Eligah Boykin Jr.
June 23rd, 2018

NOTHING BUT ECSTASY

Down in the pit of Spiritual Poverty where all
the unloved
and unwanted
and uncared for
ruminate about the doubtful advantages of corporeal gifts
owed to the throw of the dice
that is augured through genetic calculations
there were those who held fast to a shining image
that issued forth from the bowels of their being
indistinct and unrefined for all its value

Phantoms arose out of the tar pits and the fetid swamps
hoary as the wisps of vapor that arise from within
the morning darkness
launched upon simmering waves of heat
yet to take hold of the Earth
dismembered and dispersed pieces of dreams
gathering and reforming
to find purchase enough
to stride forward into the Land of the Known

In such a manner as this she arose
out of the mighty detritus that houses
and nurtures the countless untold explosions
of those seedlings seeking escape with all the others
serving their prison sentence to the verdict of gravity
and making subsistence on little more than sunlight
and water
and the sugars that sweetened their tomorrows

Comely as she was yet and still she appeared to be
a work in progress
filling out the exact specifications of that blueprint
that required the harmony of proportions growing forth
into the sensuous panoply of ovoid and spherical dimensions
and he marvelled
while his pulse quickened
at her aspect and form
that promised nothing but ecstasy

-- Eligah Boykin Jr.
February 16th, 2017

ORGIES OF DESTRUCTION

We sat in front of the screens of distraction
dining on the blood and gore meeting
the nationally approved standards required
as the soul food of the nation and there
being an over abundance of this crispy crunchy
nail-biting course of consumption fit to encourage
the digestion of our own undoing and disaster we pigged out

When the duly deputized members of the warrior class
let everybody know they were having a party
we came looking askance at the tables piled high
with the harvest of bodies now ripe collateral damage
and it really looks like there will be plenty of side orders
to take home in a doggy bag as the party-goers coming
and going become willing gluttons gorging on fresh death

Our minds are bred on this tasty diet of downfall
as we smirk with smacking lips grateful to be
the one doing the eating rather than being served
up as just another item on the menu and glad
to be ineligible for the nomination of what's for dinner
in the alley of annihilation where the dumpsters are filled
to brimming with the left overs from these orgies of destruction

-- Eligah Boykin Jr.
July 23rd, 2017

OUTLAWS OF THE MIDNIGHT SHIFT

Surviving the artificial selection of the Middle Passage
many of the brightest, bravest and the strongest along
with those chosen few standing up as representatives
of the highest brand of leadership under fire and chains
and the lash of the Euro-American Empire lay their plans
upon the altar of he who is the leavening agent of all outcomes

Arising beneath the full moon foraging for a hiding place
and taking care to only raise up to full height once the sound
of barking dogs has faded into the night fugitives for Freedom
let fall their footsteps in the silence of the darkness and flee
between the vast and myriad rows of King Cotton's killing fields
following the lights in the sky spilling forth from the Drinking Gourd

Nobody knows how many lit their lanterns in order to serve
as that point of illumination calling the runaways to a safe haven
and a brief respite from the punishing trek of hundreds of miles
again and again across state borders and the scarred flesh and backs
of companions serving now as the living links over that burning
spiritual desert where anguished cries die stillborn in the womb

When finally the small party came to that place where the shimmering
waters shattered and sparkled in the kiss of the Sun and parted
the land for all arriving boats to depart and be away from the horror
and the ghastliness that yet still stains the minds and the hearts and
the souls of those committed to abase themselves for the sake of Empire
their open hands became upraised and God accepted their answered
prayers

-- Eligah Boykin Jr.
March 20th, 2015

OVERCOMING DEGRADATION

What was the product of those endless nights
of study
and what was there to show now that the
midnight oil
was nothing more than a vapor drifting
on the air
a nameless something unable to be grasped
for all
its vaunted worth as an aid to the determined

Behind the podium he grappled with an uncontrollable
urge to pee
on himself
and always seemed on the verge of self-abasement
somehow
in a society that found its empowerment
in his oppression and the exploited energies
of those forced to fall to their knees
in order to worship what they hated

When he writhed
wrapped up in the coils
of his own frustration
now the compound interest
of thousands of encounters
where his inadequacy and insecurity
stared him in the face
the outlets he craved closed up
tighter than a whore's padlocked pussy

Everyone waited or stood idly by
expecting him to lose his mind
any minute now
or take that final step
to complete his own ruination
with a handshake and a smile
and so he held onto the mental image
picture of him now overcoming degradation...

-- EligahBoykin Jr.
November 13th, 2017

PARADOX OF PLENTY

Now that Mobil has discovered
oil Obiang has nothing to do
but count his blessings in cold hard cash
while taking his sweet time
to spread the wealth amongst the people

The immigrant workers from Liberia
and Cameroon need not sweat
as much on the cacoa and coffee
plantations now that black gold
is more valuable than clean drinking water

Let the Bantu and the Fang people
think small on their cocoa farms
after pushing the Pygmies aside to
the fringes of society and doing
what they can to make Rio Muni grow and prosper

Recovering from Nguema's neglect
nearly everyone seems to be
able to read and write these days
and stemming the tide of malaria and measles is
less engaging that celebrating the feats of "Eric the Eel"...

-- Eligah Boykin Jr.
April 14th, 2018

PATTERNS OF SURVIVAL

A study devoted to the absence of your touch
the missing virtue of your flowering sacred kiss
devoid of the flooding affirmation and warmth of
your kind embrace leads as all such studies must
lead to the barren ground where the empty shells
of shrunken seeds are swept away in the fury of the
wind and turned aside from a natural nesting perched
upon the brow of a rain drenched Earth admitting sunlight
and the green radiated sugars collecting upon the mirrored
face of the swirling azure pool so denied its season of sprout

The hand that breaks free of the shackles that words
can forge upon the mind and soul flexes a power that
dims the supremacy of the image scratched in the dust
with dried, withered sticks dipped in the excreta of those
winged things that have left in flight barely a trace of their
own shadow as they soar without pause to a more favorable
season awaiting their arrival in the fixed turn and eternal round
of the wheel of Life arrayed almost as Joseph was in the feathery
cloak of many colors revealing to this all and ever expanding eye
the dripping and flashing pressured glimpse of patterns of survival

-- Eligah Boykin Jr.
September 1st, 2015

PEACE FOR PELE'

Santos arrived at Lagos International
and the Giants of Africa celebrated throughout
all the land that Pele' was in town
now the Green Eagles would have their chance
to match their feet and kicks against the best

Football took the center stage over Civil War
and juntas and Biafrans bombing Obagie village
as Lagos City Stadium and the Ogbe Stadium
in Benin packed in all the farmers and the herders
and the fishermen these could contain to cheer the matches

Hausa rubbed shoulders with the Igbo
and watched the Yoruba rise to applaud
the two goals scored through the champion
devices of that master footballer from Brazil
and for a fleeting time the stench of war was less foul

Now what will the Sun and the Moon oversee
will Democratization one day redeem
the fallen victims of warfare starved and ravaged
with disease in the millions and can Goodluck Jonathan
and Muhammudu Buhari preside over the price of Independence?

-- Eligah Boykin Jr.
March 21st, 2018

PIECES OF TRUTH

We were reading the essays of Shaaban bin Robert
when this herd of wildebeast passed before us
across the wide expanse of the Serengeti as I turned
to Aailyah who was lying on her stomach while
the wind fluttered through her hair and the pages of her book

The Father of Swahili held about as much importance
to me as the tea fields of Tukuyu but it being
required reading we buckled down and backpacked our way
forward to some place where we could be alone
with our thoughts and our books and school assignments

Aailyah wanted to visit a church somewhere nearby
in Dar es Salaam on Sokoine Drive I think
and I being Muslim just wanted to throttle the bike
and make our way to the National Mosque
in Dodoma where we could take pictures for our papers

She scolded me for daring to use one of our photographs
of Nyerere Bridge in Kigamboni as a bookmark
for my reading but I shrugged and flipped my hand at her
there would always be new opportunities to document
that as well as Nkrumah Hall at the University of Dar es Salaam...

-- Eligah Boykin Jr.
June 27th, 2018

PORT OF DJIBOUTI

Andreas sat on a crate
carefully unwrapping a samosa
as he squinted into the Sun
watching indolently as the cargo ships
sailed in and out from Ethiopia

The rusted barges and terminal containers
barely made a ripple in the waters
of the port stuffed to their gills
with whole cocoa beans and cocoa paste
and barrels of petroleum and natural rubber

A blue-naped mousebird perched
high upon the main mast of one
of the export vessels loaded down
with coconuts, Brazil nuts and cashews
as he wiped the taste of spiced potatoes from his mouth

He watched an Atar man
sitting off to the side cross-legged
and murmuring with closed eyes
some kind of poem about love and passion
while he heard the oud being plucked
in this Port of Djibouti

-- Eligah Boykin Jr.
April 11th, 2018

POWERS OF INFINITY

All black holes being equal
some galaxies are more expanding
than others around these spaces
and dymaxion geometry to the contrary
what is inside does not always exactly match
the vapor trails out among the stars
where whirling bits of gas and dust
clash and smash and dash among the asteroids
and the planets dragging around moons
within the orbital mix of their interstellar journey...

Towards where will we ever go
and from whither and whence did we come
to find ourselves the fallen in a self-perpetuating trap
enfolding and outfolding matters of chaos
growing ever more engrossingly solid around
the frame and the nature of our being
until we are one with the momentum rushing
and surging forward to the appointment
of some unknown time and destination
among the countless rocks hurled by the powers of infinity?

-- Eligah Boykin Jr.
October 3rd, 2018

PROCESSION OF MIRACLES

Finally the best came out of his mess
and the long awaited moment where his life
went into cruise control brought speed
to his need for God to do all the rest

That unbroken streak of indebtedness
vanished with the wave of some invisible
magic wand and suddenly he was back in the black
and able to pay his way from this moment forward

The one he was on the hunt for all this time
through the prickly web of unrequited love affairs
now was seeking him out to convince him
of her devotion by any of the means necessary

There was no longer any need to sweat here
the exertion of tremendous energies were just now
making their way out of the spin cycle transformed
into the penetrating ease of reason and intelligence

Now in rapid succession he gave high fives
to every miracle that passed his way clicking
the overflowing abundance of dreams on hold
into that place where miracles no longer feared to tread

-- Eligah Boykin Jr.
December 6th, 2017

PSALM OF THE UPTIGHT KNIGHT

More to the beasts of the field and the carrion of the night
decaying in the trough at the roadside out of mind - out of sight
go these words into the wind winging it with hawks disappearing into
the light
who would have thought it - who would have bought it - or brought it
to the fight

Men and women turned their eyes from sundry appeals to reason
and pickled their favorite people prejudices with rancor and zeal for
season
these scouted for scapegoats to victimize anything that was foul to
please them
and the offal of their curses stewed in all their unrest and could not
really ease them

The lowly raised their eyes and hands skyward to a heaven built upon
greed
praying for pennies from heaven to shower and replenish their desperate
need
unaware that their unreason was the source for everything suddenly
going to seed
and that they were better served to look to their neighbors for that upon
which to feed

Outside the boundaries of their fenced abundance was the source of
their salvation
within the hands of the dispossessed now resided the true and final
rescue of the
nation
the souls of those swept beneath their feet for services rendered were
now about to fashion
a self determined return to glory with triumphant weal flooding out
justly in overdue passion

These pilgrims came from the ends of the Earth to claim and get their
right
and brought before them the flickering lamp of knowledge ascending
to the height
of all that heretofore was promised to them before it became just food
for the hungry mite
their prayers are donning the mantle of reality according to the Psalm
of the Uptight Knight

-- Eligah Boykin Jr.
December 19th, 2016

QUALITY OF DREAMS

All his life he dreamed of creating
a body of work
that would be a treasure chest
of wonderful delights
for all who dared to venture
and peer within
at the Marvels of the Human Spirit

She woke up one morning and found
him in the core of her heart
all at once a still placid pond
a meandering brook
and a roaring waterfall crashing
into the depths
of her immortal being to the tingle of her toes

The compadres saw the word and number
in the blue airy sky
and hoisted the brightly colored banners
and fluttering standards and flags
high above the carnal and violent misapprehensions
of an age cloistered in its own blindness
to announce at last the celebrations to commence

The peoples of the world discovered themselves
finding that fair exchange
that shuttled no one to the ash heap of history
or sought to bury the hard won
spiritual truths under the uneven foundations
of technological hubris
the candles of Man finally flickering with enlightenment

Nature awoke in the various savage lands
and established new harmonies
between the predator and the prey competing
for sustenance and the sovereignty
of the desert and the forest in the realms
of the kingdom at once yellowing dry and flushing
green in seasonal cooperation with the Sun and the Moon

The great thinkers of the Age now saw fit
to speculate beyond the
compound interest of the Big Bang and considered
new universes that would not
conform to the perspectives of any solitary explosion
but instead be amendable
immediately to the warp and woof of infinite thought

The source of all Life gathered its cloak about
the hoary host of those
who animated and quickened that impulse to ecstasy
existing outside the bounds of cellular division
and the flashing sparks of the neuron and synapse
and resided in some extra dimension
that voided happenstance and converted sense to extrasense

When we finally arrived we saw the horror story
in all its glorious gory details
written in the compacted and condensed matter
which the smash of clashing pain
and polar energies browbeat us into believing was we indeed
but now freed of the mystery of meat on the rocks
the Lord invited us to tea to discuss the Quality of Dreams

-- Eligah Boykin Jr.
November 15th, 2017

MIKE
←S IIb
MARO
nippy naw 9

RAIDERS OF THE LOST DREAMS

Once he handed over his fantasies of love to her
she proceeded strand by strand to weave them into
the tapestry of nightmare she owned and he felt compelled
to watch although he could leave at anytime to rise above
the mind numbing crush of their anger and hate in play

He knew he was not Christ and yet everyone was invited
to the party where his life's blood was served as the beverage
of choice and the body of his dreams scattered like crumbs
to the winds for all of those meandering past and toeing
the dry, brittle leaves of his fall beneath crunching footsteps

The midnight stroller turned up every now and then sundry
and odd litter skittering away before his stumbling steps
as he joined other parties fashioning a reasonable facsimile
of those things he envisioned and he thought belonged to him
alone but evidently were the common coinage of many minds

He sang the same old song about how his own day of triumph
was to come in unparalled bliss and unmatchable victory
knowing would show them the error of their ways
and the beauty and brightness of that rightness that eclipsed
all the vain machinations of the raiders of the lost dreams

-- Eligah Boykin Jr.
August 17th, 2017

RESPONSIBILITIES OF GIFTS

God dispenses his treasures for one great reason
and those who face that reason
find wealth without measure in the meaning of their lives
every talent is a double-edged sword
meant to heal or to wound according to appropriate uses

Every advantage has the aspect of a blessing or a curse
depending upon which side is held up to the light
and the facet that is shielded in the darkness grows
outside the awareness and ken of human understanding

No one considers the price that must be paid
with each investment of endowment
and the cost is tallied out in sin
and sacred service to the designs and aims
of the one who bestows all rewards and penalties

There are abundances everywhere swelling
to burst as growling thunder clouds
exploding showers of life to grow the Earth anew
and the opportunity of the serious moment
finds its calling in the true exercise of responsibilities of gifts

-- Eligah Boykin Jr.
November 11th, 2017

RETURN TO DIGNITY

Standing in the wings and waiting for the cue to come
that would bring her out to engage and complete the scene
somehow heretofore defying a history of misadventures and
false starts and carefully organized folly masquerading as its own
kind of reason was the air of a new character written into the script
at the last minute

The announcement of her step was light and firm and
as beckoning as the coming of those who walk among the
clouds bringing good tidings before them and in the wake
of their approach freeing malevolent men from the crushing
weight and spiraling descent unraveling from the consequences
of their own darkness

The doors everywhere about him unlocked and suddenly
he found himself holding in his hands those sundry things
that up to now he could only view through screens of some
kind or encounter thoughtfully upon the printed page with
those intoning sonorously how this misdirection was to be the
route to his salvation

But it all seemed to him to be so much desperate wandering
through the winding tunnels of a maze whose ultimate design
he was hard put to envision with enough clarity to discover and
then effect that final out into that reality which proved to him to
be only natural as his fingertips pressed upon her shining brow in
a return to dignity

-- Eligah Boykin Jr.
February 11th, 20

ROBERT CHOCOLATE BARS

Alima and Alexein departed from the Pirate Graveyard
their search for the treasure of Captain Kidd
coming to nothing as they ambled thoughtfully among
the withered headstones serenely presided over
under the soaring boughs of the baobab trees and traveller's palms
Alexein threw a pebble at a ring-tailed lemur scampering
while the couple took the paved road through
to the awaiting dugout canoes they cheerfully hailed
to ferry them away from the sand and the shores
of Saint Mary's Island their eyes teased with the flash of a whale
Hopefully their departure left them more than enough time
to travel back to the mainland before the trade winds
picked up and their arrival into the capital city of Antananarivo
would bring them to the soccer stadium just about when
the Hiragasy dancers were done and the Moraingy bouts began
Besides, Alexein knew Alima more than deserved a break
from the crowded classroom in her native village
where she endeavored to patiently teach her little charges
how to make more than embroidered tablecloths for tourists
remembering Ravalomanana as she unwrapped her Robert
chocolate bar...

-- Eligah Boykin Jr.
May 29th, 2018

ROLL CALL

"ALGERIA"
Bouteflika arose with the help of his aides
Well, let us give a sincere welcome to 'the living dead'...
"LOURENCO!"
"PRESENT FOR ANGOLA, SIR!"
"Angola has our blessings, sir."
"MASISI!"
"BOTSWANA SALUTES YOU, SIR!"
"We welcome Botswana as well,"
"NKURUNZIZA!"
"HERE FOR BURUNDI, SIR!"
Hmph. Hope he's not expecting an award for just
showing up...
"KABORE!"
"BURKINA FASO IS HERE, SIR!"
Father Africa spied Thomas Sankara in the upper gallery
but made no further comment...
"FONSECA!"
"REPRESENTING CABO VERDE, YOUR HONOR!"
Father Africa let the learned scholar take his seat.
"Very well then, ... CAMEROON!"
A whole row of men, women, and children stood up
"THE PEOPLE ARE HERE, SIR!"
Hmmnn, Biya did not show, fascinating...
"CENTRAL AFRICAN REPUBLIC!"
"REPRESENTED, SIR!"
Father Africa narrowed his eyes...
"Is that you, Touadera?"
"Yes, sir!"
Father Africa gestured his acceptance of the greeting
and went on,
"CHAD!"
Delby bolted upright scolding his children
"WE ARE HERE RESPECTFULLY, SIR!"
"COMOROS!"
The musicians in the back played the National Athem

for Comoros while Assoumain proudly stood and
respectfully regarded the Presiding Officer
"PROUD TO BE PRESENT, SIR!"
Father Africa watched the ceiling lights glint and flash
off Assoumain's bald pate as he sat back down
"DEMOCRATIC REPUBLIC OF THE CONGO!"
"WE PRESENT OURSELVES, YOUR HONOR!"
Father Africa nodded at Kabila to resume his seat.
Father Africa shifted again through his papers.
"DJIBOUTI!"
"PRESENT!"
Guellah sat down again after uttering this amidst withering
stares but some general applause as well
"EGYPT!"
Anwar Sadat took to his feet to the astonishment of the
assembled party
"WE HAVE COME, YOUR HONOR!"
"We bid you a warm welcome."
"EQUATORIAL GUINEA!"
The delegation of Women and Children along with
Eric Moussabani and Paula Barita Buloya stood up
"THE PEOPLE ARE HERE, SIR!"
Father Africa patted his heart before them.
"ERITREA!"
"WE SALUTE YOU!"
Father Africa accepted this, but the mood was turning
ugly and there was grumbling among the assembly
as he waved for President Isaias Afwerki to be seated.
"ETHIOPIA!"
The Lion of Judah proudly rose to an ovation
of drumming hands and shouts of exultant triumph
Father Africa allowed for this display of emotion patiently
before at length pounding his gavel to restore order
"OUR PLEASURE TO BE HERE!"
"Duly noted, sir. We are happy to have you."
Father Africa spoke again above the back slapping
and the sight of Haile Selassie bowing and shaking hands
"GAMBIA!"
Adama Barrow stepped up and gave a curt bow.

"WE ARE HERE, SIR!"
Father Africa grunted with a smile.
"GHANA!"
Osei Tutu arose and the calls of approval became deafening
for several moments.
Father Africa heaved a sigh of relief.
"OUR BLESSINGS, YOUR HONOR!"
"Gratefully accepted, your highness."
Father Africa looked askance at his secretary and baliff
before clearing his throat.
"GUINEA!"
Alpha Conde' stood up to the applause of his entourage.
"READY, SIR!"
Father Africa turned grim as he continued –
"GUINEA-BISSAU!"
Jose Maria Vaz arose to mingled cheers and murmurs of
resentment.
"WE ARE READY, SIR!"
"IVORY COAST?"
The economist Ouattara stood up and Father Africa smiled,
"THE IVORY COAST IS HERE, SIR!"
"KENYA!"
"KENYA IS HERE, SIR!"
The worn but proud Kibaki returned to his seat.
"LESOTHO!"
Moshoeshe arose and that settled it for Father Africa.
"LIBERIA!"
"LIBERIA IS HERE, SIR!"
"THANK YOU, MADAME PRESIDENT!"
Ellen Sirleaf sat down and Father Africa went on...
"LIBYA!"
"PRESENT, SIR!"
Father Africa was heartend to see King Idris here
representing instead of Gaddafi for reasons that were
mysterious even to him...
"WHO IS HERE FOR MADAGASCAR?"
"I AM, SIR."
Father Africa could barely conceal his surprise.
"Zafy, is that YOU?"

"Yes, sir."
"God be with you then..."
"Thank you, sir."
Father Africa sighed as he came to Malawi knowing
that the youth of that nation was yet to seize
the spirit of its own country for the good of the people
"BANDA!"
"MALAWI IS HERE!"
Now came Mali, according to his notes...
"TRAORE!"
"WE ARE HERE, SIR!"
Mauritania must be next -
"AZIZ!"
"HERE, YOUR HONOR!"
The lady from Mauritius rose even before
Father Africa raised his gavel to speak
"MAURITIUS IS HERE, HONORABLE SIR."
How like her to make sure she got in the first word!
"Thank you, Madame President Garib."
"NYUSI!
"REPRESENTING MOZAMBIQUE, SIR!"
"NOTED, PRESIDENT NYUSI..."
Father Africa shuffled through his notes for the next
delegate on the roster... he narrowed his eyes... yes,
that would be Namibia...
"GEINGOB!"
"HERE, SIR!"
"ISSOUFOU!"
"NIGER IS HERE!"
So it would appear... Father Africa cautioned the secretary
and the baliff to let the Nigerian delegation wave its banners
and its flags grumbling under his breath how you could always
depend on Goodluck to do something flamboyant these days
"JONATHAN!"
"ARISE, O COMPATRIOTS!"
Father Africa rapped his gavel and admonished the crowd with
a stern, stony expression...
"NGUESSO!"
"PRESENT, SIR!"

"AMADOR!"
"MOST DEFINITELY, SIR!"
Father Africa waited for the applause to die down once more
as the self styled 'King of Slaves' resumed his seat
"MICHEL!"
"I AM HERE, SIR!"
Good. At least someone was able to tear themselves away
from all that trouble down in those islands...
"MARGI!"
"PRESENT, YOUR HONOR!"
No, Milton, reflected Father Africa, the honor is ours...
"MOGADISHU!"
"AT YOUR SERVICE, HONORABLE SIR!"
Father Africa noted the popularity of these chaps as he sought
to restore order in the hall
"MANDELA!"
"UBUNTU, FATHER AFRICA!"
The gavel pounded amidst wild cheering...
"GARANG!"
"A PRIVILEGE AND AN HONOR, SIR!"
Father Africa gestured to John to be seated hoping he kept
his feet on the ground this time...
"ZAHIR!"
"PRESENT, SIR!"
Well, and why not? Father Africa chuckled as the contralto voice
filled the spacious and drafty room...
"MSWATI!"
"HERE, SIR!"
Nowhere was it written no Kings allowed, I suppose...
"MAGUFULI!"
"WISDOM IS FREEDOM, SIR!"
Hmph. We will see about that. Father Africa pounded down
the gavel to silence the cynics...
"TOGO! WHO SPEAKS FOR TOGO?"
Olympio bustled into the hall to the applause and the approval
of the entire body of representatives.
"I DO, SIR!"
Father Africa nodded solemnly without betraying a flicker
of a smile and directed Sylvanus to find

his seat without anymore undue melodrama and commotion
"MARZOUKI!"
"HERE, SIR! REPRESENTING THE TRUTH AND DIGNITY
COMMISSION!"
Father Africa duly noted this and waved the representative
to be seated once again...
"BOTE!"
"HERE, SIR!"
Thank God Amin was still on the run...
"KAUNDA!"
"HERE, SIR!"
About time. Thought he would never make it, mused
the Presiding Officer...
"MUGABE!"
"HERE, SIR!"

Father Africa grunted as he came at last to the end of the list...

Father Africa pounded his gavel with finality before all
the delegates came to order and attention and
ceremoniously cleared his throat before the assembly so
that silence reigned as his voice echoed and reverberated
across the vast sepulcheral chamber of this moment of note

Father Africa looked with keen eyes at this assorted crew
of scholars, freedom fighters, thugs, cutthroats, clowns,
thieves, saints and true statesmen and scanned the gallery
spotting Haley and Gadaffi, Arthur C. Clarke and Nkrumah,
Biko and Sagan and he smiled to see even Marcus Garvey waving
him a salute while munching on sambusa from on high

Father Africa cleared his throat for the third and final time
"Gentlemen," he began, "welcome to the First Continental
Congress of the United States of Africa... or perhaps the
Confederated Commonwealth of African States... this is
what we have gathered here to decide right now..."

The chair recognized an objection to the very titles of these
proceedings themselves and Father Africa knew that this
vast undertaking more fit for men of stout heart than any other
as a kind of Manhattan Project for the Soul was a tale of action
and adventure that was at last underway for the whole world to join...

-- Eligah Boykin Jr.
July 5th, 2018

RIGHTEOUS AND HUMBLE

Nowhere in this world is anyone truly alone
caught in the web of forces that is this universe
flawed and on the mend supposedly recycling
writhing souls feeling at their core unqualified
for further adventures in the realm of reverse mechanics

When triumph comes knocking at the door
of undoing sometimes it can catch you off guard
but you are advised that in such cases to check
the identification badge so whether or not this be
a stranger to these premises pray bring him some refreshment

Set the table when you can to receive other favored guests
because you never know who just might stop by
in the middle of the afternoon so stock up on the mulberry
wine and bread and apples and figs and cheese for
that meeting that goes on into the wee hours of the morning

No matter how events may serve to enlarge your presence
do not be hypnotized by any of the flashing lights
that surround you to make center stage the place where
now you stand to command your destiny for weal or for woe and
remember never was it all about you as you stay righteous and humble

-- Eligah Boykin Jr.
June 4th, 2017

Idea compliments of Ilyas Bilal

SALVATION AND RUINATION

Sooner or later the whole world was going to wake up
and smell the petroleum and realize with a shimmering
flash of sunlight that the Fossil Fuel Age was over and done
with long may he rest in peace and let us give a great big hand
to all that black gold that set our feet upon the path of the Industrial
Revolution bidding us to bow mighty low at the altar of ol' King Coal
so that we can say a little prayer for the merry ol' souls who bore their crosses
of black lung and emphysema and brought up out of the mines everything a body
and a world needs to produce cancer from the waste in the air and the water and the soil

Time would tell how the nations of the world collected twenty
thousand pieces of flotsam and jetsam out of the low earth and
geosynchronous orbits and retooled and recycled all the available
space junk through the Santa Claus Machine to provide this year's
Christmas presents for girls and boys everywhere pardoning the fact of
of whether or not they were naughty or nice to their parents and grown
folks packing up their goods and undies and making a bee line for the nearest Space
Elevator to launch from the local Space Platform for that hot vacation spot on Mars
or the outer rings of Saturn without a moment to ruminate on their salvation and ruination

-- Eligah Boykin Jr.
May 21st, 2017

SEARCHING FOR IDEAS

Blazing the trails of his imagination
on a constant walkabout
into parts and realms unknown
unable to communicate
what exactly he saw lying ahead for him
as it was hard to make out
the vague and indstinct shapes and figures
enshrouded in the gathering fog
of the unknown without even the lights
of the city to serve as beacons
and a glowing compass to this dedicated trek
he was determined to see through
to the homecoming of awaiting riches
of body and mind and soul
and he felt his footprint establish itself
on the incline of something
that might prove later to be the moral
high ground in the clearing and
the coveted award which always seemed
to elude him while searching for ideas

-- Eligah Boykin Jr.
December 15th, 2017

SECOND NATURE

During the season without rain
the vast bare fields go dry
in Rwanda and stunted crops of maize
lie scattered in the scorching heat
unable to fulfill their destiny of harvest

Farmers abandon their seeded furrows
for other means to provide their families
daily bread and will trek to where the tourists
congregate to drum and practice the intore
dance for the going price of admission

There may be work to be done paving
the roads between Kigali and Butare or
on one of the coffee plantations or maybe
even the resorts of Lake Kivu will need extra
hands for the mountain gorilla tracking coming up

This year the drought stretches its gnarled bony
fingers over all the land and touches everyone except
the people near the pipes and canal coming from the River
Muvumba and in that Nyagatere District the capsicums
and melons are ripe from the green irrigation of a second nature

-- Eligah Boykin Jr.
December 9th, 2017

SERVICE INSTEAD OF LEADERSHIP

The strong young man
made his way to the podium
setting his binder down
and he began to speak
on the mysteries and varieties
of leaders and their qualities
little did he know
that in this classroom of renowned
leaders of the community
he would soon be the detonator
on a ticking cultural time bomb

Mystified as to what
he appeared to have walked into
he doggedly proceeded on
until he knew how a pin cushion
must inevitably have felt
while the steady stream of jibes and jabs
pricked the stuffings out
of him and the limits of his understanding
as those shouldering responsibilities
seemed not to realize he was like them
only here to serve
something greater than himself and to answer
the call that comes
to all able to choose service instead of leadership

-- Eligah Boykin Jr.
December 21st, 2017

SHAKA ZULU DOWN

Born without a home and forced to wander despised
from kraal to kraal as the one without a father disgrace
the only cloak for you and the mother who bore you and
fighting for a dignity that seemed always to be out of reach
as the natural entitlement of tribal bonds what does a born
killer kill to replace that which has been murdered deep down
within him and where do the cast out run and under what does
the beetle hide when the phantoms are not all in your mind and
everybody is out to get you in hopes of keeping the coming prophecy
from being fulfilled in the malevolent depths of your sharp narrowed gaze

How does a man wielding the short spear of death in combat
force himself so firmly into the imagination of his own people
so as to leave them crushed beneath his indelible bloody imprint
of slaughter and yet hear them singing his praises and whispering
his name as the Founder of the Zulu Nation that bathed in its own
blood organized this Empire as vast as the desert in it's ruler's heart
and yet as palpable as Nandi's love or Fynn's colonial machinations still
what is this chain reaction sweeping whole peoples across the sand
and into
the wind as the kings of the earth stab and stab again to bring Shaka
Zulu down

Eligah Boykin Jr.
January 16th, 2016

SIGNS TO POWER

Out of nowhere the unexpected happened
and here and there people started coming
to him for the answers to their problems
while he found much to his sudden dismay
that he could provide more positive solutions
than ever before to an unending stream
of mystifying questions coming his way

Uncommon and rare flashes of anger
brought prompt and uncontested compliance
something out of the ordinary in his life
and times as he was quick to note
while crossing the 't's and dotting the 'i's
on instructions given in more and more
minute detail to eager minds willing to grow

Humor and vitality still held its sway
as people shared the maturity
of their well-developed points of view
and found themselves invited by serendipity
to that sweet threshold where they arrived
to solve their own problems exclaiming
how out of nowhere something unepected happened

-- Eligah Boykin Jr.
August 13th, 2017

SOUL AND GOAL

Deep down beyond the gravitic forces
of this world
a mote of dust within the swirling ocean
of this galaxy
which is merely a spinning disc amongst countless
in this universe
he went where the Bantu and the Bushmen
would not go
and found within the mysteries of the human cell
treasures of renewal
where the brightness of youth glowed with an eternal light

Down past even the diamond mines and away from
the oil fields
into the caves of darkness where the Kings of Ndongo
dare not go
he laid siege to the armies of shadows policing where
the people dwelt
since snapping the reins of the Portuguese
and coming out
of the great famine and the drought to new and unknown
adventures in freedom
unforseen to even Queen Nzinga in Luanda

Past the minefields of the Angolan Civil War
he gingerly proceeded
knowing little more than the average citizen
where to step
around the potholes and the broken asphalt
discouraging the tourists

and providing a formidable challenge to even the
sure of foot
but on he strode in triumph over measles and yellow fever
completing the trek
through eighteen provinces coming at last to the monument
of Agostinho Neto

-- Eligah Boykin Jr.
January 25th, 2018

SOUL FOOD

Somehow he survived the subtle and benign censorship
of all those among his family and friends who did not come
alive upon partaking the fruits of his spirit and the works of his
soul and discovered much to his astonishment that kindred spirits
can be found in all the oddest places there are on the planet

Everyone was bent on becoming their favorite piece of eye
candy complete with body piercings and the appropriate tattoos
and seemed to be following the dictum that presentation is everything
as one strictly observes the codes of decorum concerning gift wrapping
whether or not there was anything left to be put inside the box

But our wayfarer just wanted to be clean and neat and vied
whenever he could for the rites of purification in all these things
that mattered between souls in the flux and brightened at the prospect
of becoming one and whole with the sacred geometry of the universe now
spawning new dimensions in all directions coming around the bend

The more he labored for transcendence the more space he found
all about him and the sweeter the air became to breathe and he dug
in for the hike to the summit in his hob nail boots moving at the speed
of seven leagues breathless and stumbling up until finally he came to
that
place where they served steaming hot his favorite kind of soul food

-- Eligah Boykin Jr.
July 15th, 2016

SPEED OF THOUGHT

There was a higher and better reality
than ever he knew or experienced
or endured
a swifter realization of dreams
akin to the instantaneous transformation
of love into reality
without the trauma and the drama
There was a better rhythm to the tune
of life and a swing nearer
to the aim of endless graduation
and the name of that tune
was to imagine it and be it
right on up the Ladder of Life
resounding and echoing the grandest feeling
of the best the spirit has to offer

There came to all enlightened minds
inspiration from the future instead
of the past
a seeing somehow over the horizon
and through the vanishing point
where the rich bounty of goods
reappeared in great profusion and
without conclusion with the speed of thought

-- Eligah Boykin Jr.
August 20th, 2017

Jada
Willis

STOMPIN' DOWN THE DOOR

There are some things no man can give
and the fugitive and the pilgrim banging
against the doors of the heart and fate
seek in vain for riches and treasures
in the halls of violent regard as the chests
within its rooms yield to temptation
nought but cobwebs and dust to grimy fingertips
as hands fumble with confusion in all the wrong places
and even doors cracked wide open stand only
to reveal what no earthly key can unlock

But still the stout of heart will at last try
their shoulders against the formidable
obstacle whenever the opportunity presents itself
unaware that there are other measures
gentler in nature that can turn clenched fists into
open palms releasing hawks and ravens
and doves flapping skyward with eagles for lands
where the stern face of force is opposed
to none other than the desperate pleas of those
whose prayers resist them stompin' down the door

-- Eligah Boykin Jr.
December 20th, 2017

STONE OF POSSESSION

The children wandered and marched like prison inmates
into the National History museum to see
a thing that was called the Stone of Possession wondering
what that was all about and why on Earth
would anyone need to place a paper weight on an island

No one found it necessary to convince Captain Morphey
of the logic to be found in moving this masonry block
to perch upon a granite boulder for all to see and there
were those who could see his joy and relief in getting
this thing off his ship to rest for good on Mathe' island

Once the playground of pirates and colonists alike whether
from France or England Vasco De Gama could hardly
have imagined that one day royalty of every stripe would be
down here on these granitic and coralline islands numbering
beyond one hundred filled with giant turtles and paradise birds

What did the people possess while the rich frolicked with movie stars
and the jet set celebrated the blessings of wealth reserved
to remain in the hands of the few while the open arms of the many were
excluded and school children sought to make out with keen gazes
the Fleur de lys that was now worn away from the Stone of Possession

-- Eligah Boykin Jr.
June 22nd, 2018

STORY PROBLEMS IN GHANA

Kwadwo and Yaw considered their options
as they intently watched The Black Stars
score a late game goal that brought
the stadium goers to their feet
inspiring hopes that once again
their heroes might bring home
the cherished World Cup

Kwadwo reluctantly got up knowing
that his tutor was awaiting him
at the University of Ghana's Balme' Library
Yaw would have to text him the final score
later while he crammed
for his examinations
in Basic Information Technology

Yaw grunted farewell to his friend
while his eyes never left the screen
he could relax now that his shift was over
his mind still glutted with those empty boxes
rolling down the conveyor to be
filled with smart
phones and tablet computers

Constantly Yaw debated with Kwadwo about
the merits of their endeavors for higher education
there was no denying the prestige of attending
the oldest University in Ghana
the Alma Mater of Kofi Annan
but even as Kwadwo was mastering
his story problems elite students
such as Yaw

were finding themselves irresistibly
drawn to the
Kwame Nkrumah University
of Science and Technology
for better
or for worse

-- Eligah Boykin Jr.
April 30th, 2018

STUDIES IN KHARTOUM

Khalida departed the University with full honors
a graduate of medicine and a source of pride
to her countrymen as a Sudanese woman who followed
her dream to become a doctor and made herself an
inspiration to those who wished to rise through higher learning

Since the day she was a little girl and Sudan won
its independence she dreamed of the day
she might serve to minister to the ills of the nation
and bring a soothing balm and helping hand
to the open wounds that were the fruit of Sharia Law

Now that she was recognized as the first woman Doctor
in the history of the Sudan she was aware that
she could work to lift the minds of men out of the cruelty
and above the brutal justice that was known to come
with stoning and the whip and crucifixion for social offense

Standing at that place between the Blue and the White Nile
she contemplated how she might end the hunger
in her land that she knew could erupt at any time into civil war
blotting out the sun and all the hope for progress
beyond armed conflict and slavery owing to studies in Khartoum

-- Eligah Boykin Jr.
June 26th, 2018

SUNSHINE IN MOROCCO

Fatima al-Fihri meandered through the ancient Roman ruins
of Volubilis thoughtfully reflecting upon
the ceaseless interaction and conflict between Force and Ideas
as she descended the shallow slope
under the Zerhoun Mountain overlooking the rolling fertile plain

Volubilis was no more despite the best efforts of the Berbers
and the Romans and stones from its basilica,
its temple and triumphal arch could even now be found
in the buildings of Meknes these days
the excavated and reconstructed houses merely relics of the past

While what Fatima vowed daily to fast for in the time
of Ramadan was even now flourishing
in Ifrane and still accommodating a growing population
of worshipers and refugees from distant lands seeking
spiritual solace and enlightenment in her Mosque and University

Maimonides owed her thanks along with Leo Africanus
Abul-Abbas, Muhammad al-Fasi, the historian Ibn Khaldun
and the astronomer al-Bitruji for founding a center of learning
where all were welcome to matriculate and even Pope Sylvester
gave prayers of gratitude for this woman pleasing to Allah

-- Eligah Boykin Jr.
June 19th, 2018

TALES OF THE GREEN MONKEY

Abdoulaye patted me on my fur
my golden-green hairs prickled
at his touch and I wondered how
he came to decide to bring me
to this wrestling match in the sand

Of what moment was it to me
who between Karamo and Bala
ended up being pushed to the length
of this pit in the hot broiling sun
and thrown amidst the howls of the spectators

I cringed at this unnecessary exercise
of sweat and muscular force
with half a mind to scamper off
the perch of Abdoulaye's shoulder
but for the rice and peanuts to be found in his palm

The tourists were intermingled here cheering
amongst the farmers and the fishermen
for the selected man of their wager
while I heard the voices of classroom children
sift the facts from the truths in Alex Haley's ROOTS...

-- Eligah Boykin Jr.
April 29th, 2018

THE ADVENTURES OF THE BLACK PHOENIX

Our brother in Christ
took his pacifier
out of his mouth
inside a wonderful childhood
and trusting in the Lord
stumbled forth to live
his dream with a beautiful wife
fathering his one and only son
who became a man and a Marine
while he endured a life
that long ago transformed itself
into the suffering and pain and misery
of one bereft of everything according
to the equal and opposite edict
of Newton every second of every minute
of every hour of every day of every
month of every year of every decade
a challenge and a test to his ability
to be the faith beyond walking and talking
and the manly reserve of physical prowess
while he grasped at moments of joy
with feisty pugnaciousness
clutching these precious nuggets of gold
in both fists with a nod
to Bruce Lee and Jim Kelly while life
kept dunking his head into a vat
of water like Sho' Nuff from THE LAST DRAGON
and asking him 'WHO'S THE MASTER?'
until he proudly raised his head in glowing
triumphant exaltation and relief

and declared 'I AM THE MASTER!'
and then did a twirl
and dancing away with Michael Jackson
got on down the road to begin
THE ADVENTURES OF THE BLACK PHOENIX!!!

-- Eligah Boykin Jr.
October 13th, 2018

THE COLOR OF IMAGINATION

We discovered in the flash of a sudden embrace
a solution that was standing
out there in the bright sunlight all the time
and another of the countless examples

that in the end love is the answer we are looking for
in all our endeavors and enterprises
and that the final authority ratifying or declining
our proposals for greater life
is in our hearts and souls and the breath of the God
who oversees all our affairs

Light flared through the shutters lining the walls
and the breathtaking revelation
that came to them both was how good they were
for each other in a split second
of hearwarming encounter and when all the doors
that were bolted and locked
were found to be open and gathering the sunshine
everything snapped to and fell into the place
where rectitude reigns in the sanity of the right answer
squeezed through the pores of the color of the imagination

-- Eligah Boykin Jr.
December 13th, 2017

THE CRADLE OF HUMANKIND

Down in one of the caves of the place of gold
where the bones of the earliest men
are to be found sat Solomon Plaatje along with
Alan Paton and Nadine Gordimer ready
to hand Athol Fugard a cup of steaming hot tea

The current state of the country was the first topic
on the agenda now that the lily white
minority no longer controlled the majority rights
of their darker brothers and sisters from their
tower of high technology built out of blood and tears

Nelson Mandela walked the prison yard of his University
of Freedom deliberating upon the wisdom
and the means necessary to bring this House of Cards
tumbling down around the heads of state
administering luxury founded on endless drops of native sweat

Fugard blew gingerly upon his tea before sipping it while
soberly discussing with his fellow Ambassadors of Thought
the upshot of those Professors of Liberty now sending forth
their students to take up positions and seats of power
in this beloved country poised to rock the cradle of humankind

-- Eligah Boykin Jr.
June 25th, 2018

THE DARK SIDE OF LOVE

There was more to love than a box of candy
and a dozen roses sent through Western Union
there were as well those sweaty nights throbbing
in intense obsession with the image of a single
lighted face rooted implacably in the heart
and the wildness of newly discovered passion
straining at the bounds of propriety and threatening
to break free of carefully orchestrated controls
calibrated to serve as the governing forces now
switched permanently into the 'off' position

There were rivals to be overcome in many places
some in the usual haunts wearing shoes and others
more indistinct and shadowy and not to be given
import until finally emerging out of the background
to loom in the foreground as bleeding wounds that no
longer could be dismissed as shibboleths of the benighted
mind or mere grimy encumbrances of the soul to wash
away with soap and water or some other cleansing agent
and outside the sanctity of the church or official family approval
only retreats for the fugitives will shelter the dark side of love

-- Eligah Boykin Jr.
December 9th, 2017

THE DESERT EXPRESS

Kagumbo and Makayla took the Desert Express
from Windhoek hand in hand and exulted
traveling the vast space that is Namibia flushing
with a blinding speed propelling them that was
unknown to the San or Damara and Nama peoples

Zooming through the central highlands now just
this side of the skeleton coast dry and withering
hellbent for Swakopmund across the savannah
the dunes of the widening desert yawning
before them in a rush of ruddy waves of tan and gold

Kagumbo held Makayla tightly about the waist
as the cars jostled and rocked on their wheels
careening them into the thrill of the wind whistling
nearly making the memories of the Herero and
Namaque genocide whizz like a hiss from their minds

Kagumbo's eyes narrowed as he thought of the Germans
apologizing for their colonizer Bismarck and suspected
one day South Africa would step forward to heal old wounds
and settle accounts with Prime Minister Saara Kuugongelwa
or her like but patting Makayla's hands he knew it would be
a long ride before anyone finally arrived at that destination

-- Eligah Boykin Jr.
June 19th, 2018

THE GODS OF TOGO

The Gods came to Togo to conquer gravity
in all directions and encountered Man
who warring within himself for the truths
of Faith and Free Will nonetheless could
not free himself from the chains of this world

Thus Olurun shone upon the land as it became
the Slave Coast and watched the Life Force
wan as the people were reduced to goods and services
that would enrich the world in its greed
for all the wealth that this realm can bestow to its grasp

The land where the lagoons lie saw the arrival
of the Portuguese and later the Germans
but not before the Ewa came from the East and the Mina
and the Gun from the West to produce pottery
and process iron in the way of the ancient traditions

The rains would come and go as leaders rose and fell
and Sylvanus Olympio became the First President
in the era of the Independence unable to survive the bullets
of a military coup that made the Orisha weep and Shango
boil in his wrath as the people searched everywhere for its teachers

-- Eligah Boykin Jr.
June 27th, 2018

THE GOSPEL OF MICKEY MOUSE

After treading a path rife with the thorny debris
of adversity and dappled o'er with thickening shadows
barely concealing longing and regret and the lengthening
of fading hopes across the crumbling flagstones where bare
feet and those shod leave faint imprints upon the trail of eternity
he found once again the cheer of the one who greeted him in his youth

Mickey Mouse invited him once more to play with his friends
Donald Duck and Minnie Mouse and Goofy in a fold-away house
designed just for him and to the specifications of unbridled fun to be
experienced in various adventures of learning sailing away in a hot air
balloon of dizzying heightened perception waving down at the
earthbound

Who would have thought that any side road might eventually land
one's feet back upon the main path where the parade would be coming
along past this way with the dancing snake ladies and the high wire
acrobats
and fire-eaters and lion tamers and clowns with floppy shoes waving
grandly
to invite you to the never before seen presentation of this once in a
lifetime thrill

When it came time for everyone to do the Hot Dog Dance there was
nothing left for it but to hitch up one's pants and shrug one's shoulders
in rotation counterclockwise while stepping lively to strident harsh singing
off key except in the hearts of children everywhere delighting in their
giggles at
all the bright colors exploding overhead now declaring the Gospel of
Mickey Mouse

-- Eligah Boykin Jr.
August 14th, 2016

THE GREAT UNKNOWN

Down in the blackness
where nothing is known intimately
and the vacuum encompasses
everything that nature is considered to abhor
comes the drums and the voices
its chanting muffled in the folds of darkness
refusing to peel back to admit
the revelation of sight and sound bent on making
an impression through the visceral
more than any other medium of sense

Light found no place
to escape down and through the sucking hole
of time twisting space
and wandering souls at last pick up frantically
the scent of where
they first began to dive in their spinning descent
into that final void
where blindness becomes the insubstantial qualification
for aristocracy in their
zone of nowhere but the kingdom of the great unknown

-- Eligah Boykin Jr.
December 20th, 2017

THE GREATEST GOOD

Meandering along and through the roads
and streets and over the boulevards of this world
he often wondered
what scene the best and the greatest
would make in the affairs of men
and what would be the need for winged angels
or the voice of God
to come booming out of the clouds
when there was plenty to eat in good health
and clean clothes to be pressed
and shelter fit to warm the toes in the winter
and cool the brow in the summer
and places to go
where brilliant sights abounded and things to know
that would tickle the fancy
of every earnest mind with amusements and play

When he first set out in the race
tripping and stumbling over himself
and feeling some unknown hand pushing him
out in front of all the others and sweeping him up
across the finish line he swelled with pride knowing
he was the favorite of God
no matter who else denied or rejected or forsook him
and glowed with certitude
that it would all come out right in the end
with relish on hamburgers and fried chicken and lemonade all around
and toasts among family and friends for worthy accomplishments
that expanded the community welfare in every direction
on a free wheeling basis as a regular ritual of good feeling and hilarity
with an eye towards endless graduation
ascending higher and higher into the greatest good

-- Eligah Boykin Jr.
March 13th, 2017

THE ISLAND OF AMADOR

Doctor Carvalho looked around at the usual cases
that clogged the beds of the wards with malaria
and anemia now shuttled from the Hotel Residencial Avenida
and other choice places of domicile for wealthy tourists
searching through the cabinets for the medicine that cured nothing

These islands once belonged to no one until the Portuguese
landed here amomg the hawksbill turtles, the ibis,
and the giant sunbird scattering a wayward shrew here
and there while making a survey on its volcanic soil for elements
of gain as the explorers prepared the land for the undesirables

The healer prepared the thermometers and carefully unracked
the blood pressure cuffs for the daily round reflecting
how the Jews came here from Portugal and the Blacks from places
such as Angola by all historical accounts making these islands
depots for the mainland of Africa and the Atlantic Slave Trade

The pirates and the convicts became part of the passing parade
along with the Dutch and the Jewish children separated
from their parents as African slaves made Sao' Tome number one
in the world when it came to sugar but independence came
with Manuel Pinto da Costa as the image of the King of Slaves
on the money made this one place the renowned island of Amador

-- Eligah Boykin Jr.
June 22nd, 2018

THE SEARCH WITHIN

The evidence appeared to indicate
the discovery of something more
to life than falling in love with the games
that white men can invent
or reciting their idea matrices as a catechism
for success and prosperity
within the means and bounds of the Western World

There were other games to be played
across this blue and green widening expanse
of a wobbling planet with chaos at its core
and brave were the souls whose industry
was absorbed in devising occupations of play
that might birth new freedoms into view
and make the material of the dream acceptable currency

Down within every man was a source
of salvation that could not be found
in learned tomes or the lectures of the very wise
but was best known in self communion
such as those illuminated with inner knowledge
might reveal harvested from neverending
coffers overflowing with the mysterious increase of liberty

-- Eligah Boykin Jr.
April 17th, 2017

THE SECOND COMING OF MARCUS GARVEY

The fishermen on Lake Tanganyika
saw him striding forth
across their rippling shimmering waters
in black fluttering robes
his collar trimmed in green
whilst beneath the arms
and encircling the cuffs of his sleeves
crimson met the Sun

Pierre Nkurunziza halted in his speech when
he saw him coming
The supernatural judge of all our travail
walking here on air
as well as water tasked to weigh
our past and present
transgressions against his own and the nearing prophecy
of redemption and deliverance

The Tutsi militia felt the wind stir
and a blinding light
stopped them in their tracks as they shielded
their eyes in vain
he was headed for Bujumbura and Independence Square
and woe unto those
students of civil war and genocide between the Tutsi
and the Hutu as
the Twa saw the wind swirl in The Second Coming of Marcus Garvey

-- Eligah Boykin Jr.
February 10th, 2018

THE TALKING DRUMS

The Talking Drums resounded
along the Ivory Coast
as the Second Ivorian Civil War
brought blood and slaughter
to the center of the stage
despite any of the curses in French
amongst the Catholics and servants
of Allah and sundry inhabitants
worshiping the same God
and even the students
of the Universite' de Coudy
look up from their books and papers
now that their studies are punctuated
with the roar of bone-jarring explosions
leaving the evening meal of Yassa to sour
on the lips and the tongue
Mass armed conflict proving poor for the palate
and the digestion of cocoa
in whatever form it is processed and produced
for the villagers and the Capitals
of Yamoussouka and Abidjan
and the maw of the world

-- Eligah Boykin Jr.
April 11th, 2018

THE ULTIMATE PORN GODDESS

A temptress of souls
eye candy to human calculators
whose buttons she presses
with every gesture of her comely features
computing equations of lust
that she has personally mastered
to her own benefit
all the numbers seem to add up
for her every time
she moves her curves or poses her figure

Impervious to fawning worship
the inspiration of fantasies
galore in a thousand and one ways
presenting herself as available
to feasting eyes primed to dine
on her flesh more
as gluttons knowing no satisfaction
for what ails them
she kindles addictions making the lonely hearts serve
the ultimate porn goddess

-- Eligah Boykin Jr.
December 21st, 2017

THE UNITED STATES OF BEING

Down on the ground floor it appears beyond reach
as something more accessible in a dream than waking
life and beyond the thousand miles requiring the invite
of that first step as that last glance inspires one to shrug
before sighing how there was no way to what might have been

There was too much pain to the undertaking and too
many ways to veer off the beaten path and the sodden
mud of loss clung to soles of one's boots until there was a
shifting underfoot and that alarming sense of sinking down
into the abysmal quicksand where almost there found no cigar

Everything in the end hinged on finding the right question
to the right answer and hoping that was all there was needed
to part the curtains and let the Sun come pouring inside where
the gray outlines of objects in silhouette suddenly resolve into the
bright clarity of that iridescent truth in all its many webbed features

But all the wanderings in a wasteland of broken oaths
lacquered hates and sullen silences and fears still untested
in the miscalculations of Fate as well as all the time worn tales
of how I owe you because you sold me outside of expert skills makes
hover into vivid sight the recycled prestige of The United States of Being

-- Eligah Boykin Jr.
January 29th, 2017

THE VALLEY OF HEAVEN

Mswati surveyed the 1954 Buick LeSabre owned
by his late father Sobhuza the Second
and chuckled to himself wondering how such a man
with seventy wives and more than two hundred
children ever found the time to drive himself anywhere

Swaziland was a long way now from the Khoi-san
hunter-gathers and British rule these days
and Sobhuza led them well into their Indepenedence
during his long reign that all began in infancy when
Ngwane dropped dead dancing the sacred ritual of kingship

Now the fate of his developing country was finally resting
upon his shoulders here in the city of Lobamba
and an aide whispered in his ear it was time for him to depart
for the Lumkokwing University of Creative Technology
where students and faculty were even now preparing for his address

Mswati mentally reviewed his notes for the affair and hoped
that the Swazi scouts would not show up to protest
and march against him simply because he would prefer not to have
Swazi women enduring AIDS to transform this land
from a Valley of Heaven into a disease ridden Valley of Broken Men...

-- Eligah Boykin Jr.
June 27th, 2018

THEATER OF THE BODY

The world comes to us gift wrapped in multitudinous
comely features suitable for framing on the walls of our
memory banks and offers to our view all the sensual delights
sketched to full materialization
in gleaming sight
luscious sound
vivid aroma
sumptuous taste
and voluptuous contour
filling the moist palms
of grateful hands in prayer

We feel compelled to place the fruits of this world
upon the altar and the pedestal of vain hope
that we may preserve these moments and save from decay
and the natural process of rot our inheritance
due and owed to the authors of original sin
who long ago departed the perfect symmetry of God's love
for parts and places unknown...

The thrill of blooming youth ripening into all its full
dimensions throttles lust and obsession for this
earthly plane as nothing else can
and the craving to expand this phase of life into Eternity
inspires more devotion to its cause
than all the gold in El Dorado
where phantom footsteps
have been know to tread

The grace
Strength
and utility
of all physical forms
as lasting as the crystalline structure of a snowflake
dazzling as it enthralls us to seek out the source
from whence it proceeds and with unknowing gestures
causes us to grasp for answers that can only come
when the curtains close on this theater of the body

-- Eligah Boykin Jr.
February 5th, 2017

THEATER OF THE MIND

We kept receiving reports about this strange planet where
spiritual powers could be exercised to do all manner of good
involving feeding the hungry
clothing the naked
sheltering the homeless
and providing locomotion for those stranded and without
means to go where the best interests of their survival might lie
owing to that hoped for kindling of the flame that ought to light
the soul
and how reward for all this would be vituperation mixed
with spittle as well as the red stripes of torture raised to the
highest pitch of agony bearing the signature of death

We found it curious that a galactic population might exist
that relished the observation of destruction as a way to pass
the time
and whose sight
and blindness
and awareness
was best
enhanced and corrected
whenever they were addressed in anger, fear and hatred,
the tuning fork that best alerted their attention and senses
to the coming trials of their mortality
and that those who cried the loudest for new freedoms
were the quickest to see the benefits of a slave state
that the most beautiful of women secretly craved
the evil ways of men
and longed to cultivate an aspect that would seduce
the high and mighty to their will

We were taken aback and astonished at the nature
of their profitable enterprises
centering upon the unrest of all kinds of war
and lust for gain
as well as both the subtle and violent poisons
lowering their consciousness into the dark solace
of the grave and we puzzled to ourselves
as we decided to forsake their orbit
how they could ever find such entertainments
fit for the Theater of the Mind

-- Eligah Boykin Jr.
February 4th, 2017

TRANSFORMATION BEYOND TRANSCENDENCE

Everywhere he encountered in the back alleys
of post modern strife all the newly minted survivors
steadfastly holding onto all their most cherished ideals
in the enclosing darkness unaware in the growing faintness
of the light that all that lay cloistered in the fastnesses of their
hearts twas as nothing compared to the rich treasures that stretched
out before them over the horizon

Some caught sight of the ladders stretching skyward
to dizzying heights and plummeting through the death
defying abyss to the flaming core of the Earth and found
their footsteps dedicated to paths not of their own choosing
as far as they could tell in these coming and going adventures
of creation and destruction while resistance to the inner will of
their Divine Mandate proved only futile.

Their universes infolded and outfolded in the manner
of a vast egg foaming upward and sucking in its contents
the way a Santa Claus Machine of Life spews forth gifts of
all sizes for every girl and boy regardless of the color of their
past or the flashing checkerboarding of their present as they are
spilled out of the mud baths and reeking swamps into the deliverance
of a future shining with sweat

Eyes were uplifted to behold opening and closing doors
without end that spiraled into the clouds to at last embrace
a zone beyond all the dark energy and matter held in suspension
within the black vacuum where planets and stars and suns twinkled
out a mysterious code to be shared with all those crawling and creeping
and bounding away across the savannas and light filled forests scurrying
to gasp and at the last amble forth and stride at first uncertainly out of the wet
splashing of an earthly transformation beyond transcendence

-- Eligah Boykin Jr.
December 31st, 2016

TRUE INFINITE RENEWAL

There was true crime
and true confessions
and true love in the big leagues
and the big city
and jets of human potential
being spewed in all directions
three hundred and sixty degrees worth
where it does nobody any good

While deep in the heart
of the human cell
swirling within the flaming core
of all its working parts
was the universal principle of replication
a fingerprint away from the unique
geometry of snowflake dynamics producing patterns
that never again will be repeated

And so at last we come
to the badlands of Pi
where nothing returns as a recognizable paradigm
for inevitable predictable decay
and we find ourselves negotiating
an escape route between the gnashing
grinding gears of endless descent
that leads immortally to true infinite renewal

-- Eligah Boykin Jr.
December 5th, 2017

TRUTH AND JUSTICE

Down just off the southeastern coast of Africa
lies an island amongst a chain of its kind
the spawn of a volcano and unknown to human footprint
before the Arab sailors caught sight of it
with the wind at their sails and named it Dina Arobi

Here came the Dutch for the goods of the ebony trees
gambling at the game of settlement with sugar cane
and domesticated wildlife and prancing deer until all
their ventures proved no go and finally they were obliged
to abandon this place that was namd for Prince Maurice

The French decided to give this playground their trial
after the Code Noir was established the privateers
finding it a serviceable base for telling raids to make
the island a going enterprise complete with the goods
of slavery until the British landed at Cap Malheureux

After the display of Ratsitatane's head to serve
as a caution to those imported in chains from Africa
and Madagascar whose thoughts might gravitate towards
future uprisings came Mahatma Ghandi before the Father
of the Nation prepared Fakim's cachet as President of the Land

-- Eligah Boykin Jr.
June 12th, 2018

UP FROM ALABAMA

He came from a little town called Prestwick
deep down South in a place where
Black folks were always in control
and marshaled his marbles to roll across
the black and white squares of the checkerboard
letting the dominoes fall where they may
into the last rank
where leaping to score the winning basket
and limping in a trot on crutches to catch
the Crosstown bus to Robert Hall
he came at last to the endgame
where he brought the world to checkmate
and was duly crowned a king of the realm

Coming up North he brought his Mother Wit
and street savvy
barely aware he was the visceral and living embodiment
of the wisdom and the faith of
Booker T. Washington as Carter G. Woodson
passed him the baton and bequeathed to the man the task
of weaving his own strands
into the tapestry of cultural legacy
that pressed against him with more gravity than all
the Dialogues of Plato and Socrates
and the newly minted and approved techniques
of mechanical advantage that were added
to his repertoire of tools
designed to adjust and repair the cogs of a new age

Nothing came easy as the pain
crept into his bones and time and again landed him
flat upon his back to watch the less afflicted
and more spry weather their challenges upon two good legs
while in sullen silence he wrapped himself in his vicissitudes
and emerged relentlessly out of every adversity
as a man transforming his agony

into a game of catch with his sons
and a bare open lot of growing corn
as tall as an African Chieftain stands
while maneuvering the iron bars, chains and pulleys
to switch the motors of destiny
between two cars
soon to be driven into the age of Obama

Jomo Kenyatta nodded sagely and noted from on high
that at last here was a man with the right stuff
who would stand behind no lectern
or let the echo of high sounding words
be his mask
but in the African way
that flowed like a river through his blood
let the very life within him preach and teach
and set the moral high ground
for all that would come after
and his sister and his loving wife and daughter
marveled at his will to survive
as they heard the laughter of Kings all the way
from Songhai and Mali to Timbuktu
as he ascended the Stairway to heaven
to prepare Saint Peter's taxes
and sell Chitlin' Loaves in that Cabin in the Sky
explaining to Christ and all with wit to listen
how it was all just leverage
and compound interest in the end

-- Eligah Boykin Jr.
April 20th, 2017

VOWS TO KEEP

Strange how in the world of today
abounding and teeming over
with brightly wrapped things
and stuffs of barcoded material
prosperity
we here wallow in the depths
of a spiritual poverty
that gnaws like worms
at the decaying corpse
of our shattered inner peace

Here in our present times
designed to exercise those transactions
meant to feed the expeditionary forces
of the bottom line
our promises are mere trifles
to be thrown overboard
when there is rough going
and we find ourselves swearing forever
when we really mean for the fun right now

But no matter how we buy and sell
the delusions of our age
we slowly discover that some things
are not up for barter
and come with no price tag available
for the informed consumer
and bear no expiration date
even to the most discerning eye
and will not be bargained away

Such are the inner commandments
written upon the soul
that will never be abrogated by any being
even under the most dire threats
of banishment and corporeal extinction
and it is best after reading
the fine print in the contract
to carefully review
those most important things
that we have made our vows to keep

Eligah Boykin Jr.
May 27th, 2017

WAGES OF LUST

I studied arduously to win the approbation of my peers
but all my labors devoted to poring over many a ponderous
tome came to nothing as certain as the inevitable contumely
won for reasoning outside the narrow bands of all that now was
considered right and true and normal in the view of community welfare

I competed for the prizes of Life with all those who bent low
with me at the starting line and capered ahead in the first flush
of exhilaration not realizing that the determination of those ranked
beside me would have them still sweating and jockeying for an edge here
sometimes won and sometimes lost in a desperate plunge for the finish
line

I calculated vaguely for an insight into the mysteries of compound
interest and its lively play of perpetual increase and came a cropper
upon the reefs and rocky prominence of my own misunderstandings
jutting out in all the odd places where the greater truths filed down to
a smooth finish would have made a better fit in the sheen of future
success

I found my enterprises cloaked in degradation and the unknowing
assent to regulated downfall divinely timed to service the goals of even
strangers about me who found unexpected luck in my misfortune and
some
advantage owing to the default in every step of my erring ways while
I discovered
myself in a lonely hallway knocking on the Devil's door to receive my
wages of lust

-- Eligah Boykin Jr.
January 9th, 2017

WALLS OF HATE

Nowhere the travelers wandered
no matter the trail the citizens chose
regardless of the route taken
or the attractions of this lane over that one
no one could keep from running into them

The structures were crusty and hard
and unyielding to the touch and windowless
there were no borders above the floor
while beneath the ceiling the marks of blood
barely smelled smearing the liberal application of whitewash

Nobody was willing to talk
about the bodies buried under the floor
or the broken covenants that served
as the mortar along with the thick outrage
that made those bricks shoulders found hard to break

More than ever people were banging
their fists and heads against the hard
surfaces of centuries of bitter rancor
and misunderstanding unable to make a dent
in the festering and calcified crevices of walls of hate

-- Eligah Boykin Jr.
December 6th, 2017

WEATHERING HUMILIATIONS

Fighting the Status Quo proved to be a daunting task
but as he was batting a thousand when it came to this
there was nothing to do but step up to the plate and point
to the center field bleachers calling his shot and putting it there

The natives were all going wild in the Motor City as he
defied their customs and spotted the flaws in their most
cherished conventions unraveling inside out every pet idea
he could lay his hands on and exposing its underbelly to inspection

Living in a cultural puzzle box where surface impressions
counted for everything and people were known to crowd into
darkened rooms to shed tears and bark laughter at recordings of
death and destruction he was always there for the next exploding cigar

Sometimes he woke up on the wrong side of the law
and found it best to make his escape through the window
rather than out of the door the gendarmes were battering to
smithereens in their eagerness to serve him his notice of summons

But in the end the joke was on them chained as many of them
were to one side of the view that nevertheless seemed here to leave
somebody out wishing to belong within the same lanes of
narrow-mindedness
as those who appear to be exempt from the sentence of weathering
humiliations

-- Eligah Boykin Jr.
March 5th, 2017

WEST OF THE NILE

Who arrives for your oil now, Libya
seeing that the Kings of Antiquity
have come and gone across the sand dunes
of the Tadrart Acacus and the Sahara where
the footprints of the Berbers and the Carthaginians
are mingled in the sand with those bloody tracks
of conquest belonging to the Persians, Egyptians and Greeks

Are visitors still making their way to stand
before the crumbled rock strewn ruins
of the Temple of Zeus in Cyrene and who makes
their way to the sites in Sabratha
now that the Roman Empire has long ago fallen
and even the wind has ceased to faintly
whisper the clash and cries of the Bronze Age

Does King Idriss I rest easy at long last these days
knowing that Gaddafi has finally come and gone
or do the dust storms still find their way to blow foul
of Tripoli and Tobruk beyond any solace you might
find at Ghadames and Kafra where past talk of weapons
of mass destruction left a dry taste in your mouth
as you sighted for Benghazi just west of the Nile...

-- Eligah Boykin Jr.
May 12th, 2018

ZAMROCK AT VICTORIA FALLS

Better to be a farmer than a miner now that copper
prices were in a free fall
mused Chanda as he strummed his Kalindula up-tempo
to the beat of something in between
the screech of Jimi Hendrix and the squeal of James Brown

Come one and come all you will never hear this tune again
at a Mutomboko or Kuomboka Ceremony
and the seats are cheap up here in the daylight if you can
just find a ringside space this side of
of the devil's pool and try not to go over the edge...

Flashing forward from the closing day of the Olympics
1964 we just might make it to Lusaka
in the Queen's drawers where the WITCH boys are
still dancin' and the Blackfoot are still prancin'
and we're takin' over with ZAMROCK at Victoria Falls!

-- Eligah Boykin Jr. June 39th, 2018